RUN WITH THE WIND

RUN WITH THE WIND

by

Tom McCaughren

Dales Large Print Books
Long Preston, North Yorkshire,
BD23 4ND, England.

British Library Cataloguing in Publication Data.

McCaughren, Tom
    Run with the wind.

    A catalogue record of this book is
    available from the British Library

    ISBN   978-1-84262-521-7 pbk

First published in 1983 by Wolfhound Press

Text Copyright © 1983, 1984, 1985 Tom McCaughren

Cover illustration © Heidi Spindler by arrangement with
P.W.A. International Ltd.

The moral right of the author has been asserted

Published in Large Print 2007 by arrangement with
Merlin Books Ltd.

Dales Large Print is an imprint of Library Magna Books Ltd.

Printed and bound in Great Britain by
T.J. (International) Ltd., Cornwall, PL28 8RW

To my wife Fran, for her patience during those seemingly pointless family forays into the wild and the weeds on cold winter days, but above all, for the unflagging faith which she came to have in 'the foxes'; to my younger daughters Samantha and Simone, who braved the cold with us and who, by their curiosity and enthusiasm, encouraged me in a way that only children can; and to my other daughters, Michelle and Amanda, who helped me in various ways.

My thanks also to the late Tim and Kathleen Kelly (Uncle Tim and Aunt Kathleen) of Luggacurren, Co. Laois, their neighbour, the late Bill Morrin, Sr. Elizabeth of St. Paul's Secondary School, Greenhills, Dublin and all those who assisted me in the course of my research.

Contents

Acknowledgements

I would like to thank all those who responded to my inquiries about the fox, in particular the following people and organisations: Patricia Chable, Species Survival Commission, International Union for Conservation of Nature and Natural Resources, Switzerland; Dr. David Macdonald, Department of Zoology, Oxford, Chairman, Canid Specialist Group of the Species Survival Commission; Mr. W A. Jackson, editor, *Shooting Times and Country Magazine*, Berkshire, England; Mons. L. Perpere, Service Vétérinaire de la Santé et de la Protection Animales, Direction de la Qualité, Ministère de L'Agriculture, Paris; the Association des Amis des Renards, Paris; Mr. James Beecher, First Secretary – Agriculture, Irish Embassy, Bonn; Mr. Liam O'Flannagan, Forest and Wildlife Service, Department of Fisheries and Forestry, Dublin; Mr. Andrew McLean, Wildlife Branch, Department of Agriculture, Belfast; Mr. Fergus O'Gorman, Chairman, Irish Wildlife Federation; Mr. Michael Jackson, Field and Country Sports

Society, Kilpeddar, Co. Wicklow; Mr. Robin Hunt, Irish Masters of Foxhounds Association, Kilmacthomas, Co. Waterford; Dr. C.G. van Zyll de Jong, Curator, Mammalogy Section, National Museum of Natural Sciences, Ottawa, Canada; Mr. Ron Renault, Head of Publications Distribution Section, Canadian Wildlife Service, Ottawa; Mr. Paul Murray, Project Officer, Livestock and Animal Products, Agriculture Statistics Division, Statistics, Canada; Dr. Alan B. Sargeant, wildlife biologist, U.S. Department of the Interior, Northern Prairie Wildlife Research Centre, Jamestown, North Dakota, and the Dublin Embassies of Canada, Britain, France and Germany. I also found *An Irish Beast Book*, a natural history of Ireland's furred wildlife, by Dr. J.S. Fairley (Blackstaff Press, 1975), an invaluable source of information, while officials of Dublin Zoo, the Botanic Gardens and Dunsink Observatory were helpful in various ways.

ONE

Black Tip

Once upon a time in the valley of Glensinna, not far from Dublin, there lived a fox. His name was Black Tip.

In all of Glensinna, and it's a valley of some considerable size, there was no other fox with a black tip on its tail.

It is most unusual, of course, for a fox anywhere to have a black tip, but more so in Glensinna. For the valley gets its name from the Gaelic, Gleann an tSionnaigh Bháin, which means, the Valley of the White Fox.

It was Vickey, an attractive vixen, who had told the young fox he should be very proud of his black tip.

'Your father was right,' she had said. 'It does look very handsome.'

She had reflected for a moment before adding: 'And if it hadn't made you into a strong fighter, that might be you lying down there in the hollow.'

It was also Vickey who had set Fang and Black Tip thinking about the Great White Fox and the secret of Sinna.

'Man is our enemy, not each other,' she

13

had told them. 'We just can't win against him any more – we've forgotten how, even here.'

It was during a particularly hard winter that Black Tip first met Vickey.

TWO

Three's Company

A cold east wind blew in across the meadows, stirring the clumps of withered grass that rose above the patches of crisp snow. It whistled through the leafless trees at the top of the rise and ruffled the feathers of a rook that still preferred the top-most branches to a more friendly perch farther down. In the hedgerow beneath, a single robin bared his red breast to the wind for a moment before turning tail and hopping off about his business.

The wind curled through the dead leaves behind the hedge and around the foot of the trees, and now and then it flicked up a leaf and impaled it on a scraggy hawthorn branch or on a strand of barbed wire. For a moment a yellowhammer flittered through a clump of gorse, lending a flash of colour to a bush that wouldn't flower more fully until the approach of Easter. Then, sensing that the gorse was already occupied, it beat a hasty retreat.

The soft belly of the young dog fox rose and fell as he lay in the undergrowth. His

15

legs were wet and muddy, for he had travelled far, and each panted breath misted warmly for a moment before being taken away by the cold wind. There was a lean, hungry look about him, a look not accounted for by his lack of years. It had been a hard year, and it was getting harder. His black ears twitched to every sound, and the sharp, vertical pupils of his eyes missed nothing as he looked across the bleak, wintry landscape.

Above the meadow, a heron circled slowly on its big grey wings and decided there was no point in coming down to land. The stream was flowing, but under a layer of ice.

'I could have told him he was wasting his time,' thought the young fox. Not that he would have. He just felt resentful that the big bird had gone off. In fact, he wasn't really watching the meadow at all. He had been down there and he knew there was nothing in it for him. It was too cold and hard, so the snipe and the ducks hadn't come in to feed. If they didn't eat there, neither did he.

He was more interested in the house to his right. There was a stack of turf at the back, a line of washing, and a dog. There was always a dog. Not that it mattered, as the house had no hens that he could see. What held his attention was the brightly-lit room.

A fire was burning in the grate, and a man

and woman and several children were sitting around a table eating. The young fox licked his lips at the sight of the food, but it was the brightly-coloured lights flashing on and off that caught his eye. Tempting though the food was, the flashing lights stirred an even deeper instinct in his mind. Somewhere in his sub-conscious they awakened the realisation that the time of greatest danger in his year had come. He may not have understood that for humans the flashing red lights signalled peace and goodwill. He did know that for him they heralded the days when man would deal out most death to his fellow creatures.

The young fox eased himself up, and with a flick of a tail that was tipped with black, turned around and headed for the high country.

For what seemed many days, the clear frosty air echoed to the sound of gun-fire as the shooters searched out the lowlands. Above it all, Black Tip watched and listened. How was he to know that these shooters were not after foxes, but pheasants, and snipe, and ducks and rabbits? All he knew was that when they came upon a fox, they killed it. Why they did so, he had no way of knowing. The farmers would shoot at a fox if it was after their hens, and in a way he could understand that. But what had the fox done to these people, or for that matter, to the men who set traps for it in the hedgerows?

Whatever it was, Black Tip had to use all his wits to avoid the shooters. This he did by hunting at night and sitting tight in the daytime on some high spot where he could watch them return to comb the marshes and the meadows. That way he could be long gone if they should happen to approach his hiding place.

As the days passed, something else was beginning to occupy the young fox's mind besides the primary sense of survival. The mating urge was starting to stir within him, and he longed for the company of a vixen. Yet times were hard for vixens too. Man didn't seem to care what kind of fox he killed, vixen or otherwise, and the she-foxes were now scarce.

Strangely, it was the shooters who unwittingly provided him with a mate. He was watching them striding through the meadows. There were few, if any shots, and he knew it was because there had been a heavy frost during the night. The snipe were not there, but on some distant slope where the wintry sun would release a stream from its icy grip and allow the long bills to probe the mud for worms and other food. He would love to have known the whereabouts of that slope, just as much as the shooters, but all creatures have their secrets, and

18

today this one belonged to the snipe.

Suddenly there was a flurry of shots, as if the shooters had been surprised by something that had invited them all to have a go. Black Tip raised his head. From his hiding place among a tangled mass of last year's growth of scutch grass and briars, he could see they had come upon another fox. Puffs of blue smoke and then sounds of shots.

The other fox zig-zagged among the rushes as it streaked away. More shots. For a moment it faltered. Was it hit? No, probably just a stumble. A parting shot as it drew out of range. Now it was coming towards him. Would it draw them on to him? He made to rise. But wait. He felt a sudden surge of excitement run through his body, and he was glad he had held his ground. This was no dog fox coming towards him. This was a vixen.

Black Tip was lying in a bramble thicket on a part of the hillside that rose out of the reach of cultivation. More brambles sprawled to his right, together with some uprooted tree-stumps where the farmer had tried to clear the land and failed. To his left a shallow stream that dribbled down the surface of the hillside seeped slowly beneath a covering of ice. Just below him was a secluded hollow. Part of it was matted with a patch of wilted reeds and the rest was covered with layers of

19

withered grass spiked here and there with dead white stalks of hogweed. When the vixen reached the hollow, he knew she would be well out of the shooters' sight and it would be safe to approach her. Patiently he watched as she made her way up the hillside, pausing every now and then to make sure she wasn't being followed. Her progress was slow. Eventually she made her way up over the edge of the hollow and lay panting in the long grass.

So intent was the vixen in glancing back over her shoulder at the shooters that she hadn't noticed the young dog fox. Now as she became aware of him, she was glad she had come upon one of her own, for she too had experienced a lean and difficult winter since her last cubs had matured and struck out on their own. Black Tip eased himself up and stepped out to approach her. It was only then he became aware of a movement to his right, and realised he had company. He had been so pre-occupied watching the vixen that he hadn't sensed the presence of another dog fox, and it annoyed him intensely, partly because he had been neglectful, a mistake that in other circumstances could have cost him his life. He took another step towards the vixen to show he was laying claim to her and to warn off his adversary. The other dog fox rushed forward to dispute the claim. He was a big fox, strong, probably older, and with fangs that suggested he was a fierce fighter. Black Tip turned to face him.

Below them, the vixen licked her right haunch and jerked back her head to watch as the two dogs closed and locked in a snarling ball of fury. Turning, twisting and biting, they rolled down into the hollow, cracking and flattening the brittle stalks of hogweed. Over and over they went, into the reeds, breaking the frosted crust on the mud and mulching the half-dead leaves into a brown pulp. Black Tip felt a stinging pain in his upper lip and drew back. Furious he pounced and caught the other dog by the throat. As he did so, the other fox slipped and he hurled him to the ground and held him. How long he held him, he did not know, but he didn't release his grip until the other lay still.

Feeling tired and dirty, and with blood streaming into his mouth from his torn lip, Black Tip trotted over to the vixen and nuzzled her with his nose. She accepted his approach, and he led her up out of the hollow to where the water trickled beneath the ice. It was only then he realised the she-fox was injured. One of the shooters had found his mark after all. What they needed, he thought was, clean water. He could see it bubbling under the ice. First a big bubble would get stuck. Then it would break up into numerous smaller bubbles. Gradually these would squeeze through, and once again they would form into a bigger bubble farther on. He scratched at the bubbles with his right forepaw. The vixen lay down on the ice and tried to pick the shotgun pellets from her hip with her teeth. As he watched her, his own blood tricked from his mouth and splashed on to the ice. Then, the warm blood burned its way through the ice and mingled with the bubbles for a moment before blending with the water and disappearing. Eagerly he caught the jagged edges of the ice with his teeth and ripped it open.

The water was cold and refreshing, and it cleaned and numbed his torn lip. Having let it flow around his mouth for a moment, he got up and went over to the vixen. She was having difficulty in extracting the pellets from her skin, so he lay down beside her and searched them out with his teeth. It was important that every one of them should be located and drawn out. Otherwise she would die.

The she-fox was patient. She too knew the pellets must be removed if she was to survive. It was a painful process. The pellets stung deeply, and the probing teeth even more so as each tiny ball of lead was gripped and squeezed out. Before long, his blood and her's were mingling, first on their fur, then on the ice.

By the time all the pellets had been extracted, the combination of their blood and the heat of their bodies had melted a large patch of the ice, and they were able to roll in the cold healing waters of the stream.

When they had finished, the vixen looked at him, and having observed the black marking on his tail, said: 'Thank you, Black Tip. You have saved my life.'

It was a long time since anyone had called him Black Tip with such affection, and he found it very pleasing. She was a pretty fox, he thought, small and attractive. It was her amber eyes that appealed to him most of all. There was something warm about them, something that suggested she cared.

'What will I call you?' he asked.

'Vickey,' she smiled. 'I've always been called Vickey.'

It was a common fox name, and on some was quite plain, but on her it seemed most beautiful.

'Come, Vickey,' he said, 'it's time we were moving on. We've been here too long already. I know a place not far from here where there's good cover. We can stay there until our wounds heal.'

Black Tip led the limping vixen up into the hillside until they came to an old quarry with overhanging rocks and a protective screen of gorse and brambles. He had often used it before and knew there was a ready-made den awaiting them beneath the rocks. The den was empty, and as they settled into it they found it warm and dry and sheltered from the wind. Black Tip's mouth had stopped bleeding now, although it was painful and had begun to swell. He eased his mouth down between his forefeet and watched Vickey stretch out her right hind leg and lick her wounded hip. Having positioned her leg in a way that gave her least pain, she turned to him. She could see the swelling at the side of his mouth. Bravely ignoring her own pain, and almost as if she was taking his mind off his, she asked: 'How come you have a black tip on your tail? It's very unusual.'

'Yes,' replied Black Tip, flicking his tongue around his swollen lip, 'that's what my father always said. He told me I was the only fox in the country who hadn't a white tip on his tail.'

'I think he must have been right,' said Vickey. 'I never saw a fox with a black tip before.'

'It wasn't all fun having a black tip, you know,' he told her. 'My brothers – there were four of us – they used to tease me about it. Father would nip them severely for it and tell me he thought it was very handsome, very distinguished. Still I felt a bit of a freak. For a long time I was very shy about it and played on my own. In a way, that turned out to be a good thing. I grew strong and independent. It paid off in the end. I was the only one of the litter who survived the choking hedge traps.'

'You should feel very proud of your black tip then,' said Vickey. 'And your father was right. It does look very handsome.' She reflected for a moment. 'And if it hadn't made you into a strong fighter, that might be you lying down there in the hollow.'

As they thought about the fight in the hollow, Vickey suddenly felt very unhappy.

'Why do you look so sad?' asked Black Tip. 'Are you sorry I won?'

Vickey shook her head. 'No, of course I'm not sorry you won, silly, but I'm sorry the other dog fox had to lose.'

Black Tip was puzzled. 'One of us had to lose.'

'I know, but I can't help feeling that what we did was wrong.'

'In what way? It was him or me.'

'I know, but we're living in a time when everyone has turned against us. You yourself have just said you lost your three brothers in the choking hedge-traps. I lost two of my last litter before they were even old enough to leave me.'

'What happened?' asked Black Tip softly.

'They strayed too far from the earth. They were caught and clubbed to death.'

Black Tip felt very sorry for her, yet he still didn't see what that had to do with what he had done.

'Don't you see?' said Vickey. 'It's bad enough that we're killed by man. To do it ourselves, especially at a time when there are so few of us left, that seems a dreadful waste.'

Black Tip licked his swollen lip and thought about what she had said.

'I hope you're not offended,' she went on. 'I mean, I appreciate how bravely you fought for me, and I'm glad you won, but if we continue to die at the rate man has been killing us, there'll soon be none of us left.'

In his heart Black Tip knew his mate was right. She was a compassionate creature, just as her eyes had indicated. Maybe even a bit soft, but she was right, and now he began to feel regret for the fact that he had killed a fellow fox. A fine fox he was too.

'I wonder...' Vickey began.

Black Tip raised his head expectantly.

'I wonder if he was dead when we left him?'

'The life had gone out of him when I let him go,' said Black Tip. 'It was him or me.'

'I know,' Vickey consoled him. 'You did what you had to do. But I also know you could have torn the throat out of him if you had wanted to ... and maybe, just maybe, the life will flow back into him. You've seen it happen with rabbits.'

Black Tip nodded. He recalled seizing a rabbit once and carrying it back to his earth, only to see it come back to life again and frighten the wits out of him. 'Maybe you're right Vickey,' he replied, 'but it was a tough fight. Anyway, if I didn't kill him, the frost will surely take him.'

'Then we've no time to waste,' she told him. 'Let's go and see.'

Black Tip led her out of the quarry by a different route in case a dog had picked up their scent or the smell of blood. They paused to sniff the wind. It carried no sign of danger, and slowly they made their way back down the hillside.

There was a deathly stillness as they peered over into the hollow. Nothing had changed – the cracked and crumpled hogweed where they had tumbled down the slope, the fresh brown mud among the reeds, the white belly of the other dog fox. It was plain to see he hadn't moved. Only a very thin film of ice had formed over the stream where they had washed, so the afternoon frost hadn't yet taken a firm hold.

Cautiously they approached the body. The mouth was tightly closed and they could see the teeth still gripped some of Black Tip's fur. Vickey sank to the grass and edged forward until her head was resting on the white upturned belly.

'Quickly, Black Tip,' she cried. 'Quickly! There's movement. He's still alive. Help me turn him over.'

27

Together they nudged the other fox over on his side. His legs and jaws seemed to have stiffened in readiness for death.

Vickey poked him with her nose to try and stir whatever life was left in him. He didn't move and she wondered if it was too late.

'What will we do?' asked Black Tip.

'We found the water very healing,' said Vickey. 'Perhaps if we clean him up it'll help.'

They climbed back up to the shallow stream and broke the new layer of ice that was spreading across the spot where they themselves had washed. The water seemed even colder now, but they wet their tongues and set about trying to lick some life into the still body.

'It's hopeless,' said Black Tip at last. His mouth was hurting and their efforts hadn't been rewarded with the slightest flicker of movement. Once more he went up to the hole in the ice and bathed his throbbing lip, and when he returned he sat down beside Vickey. She gave the body another nudge just in case. When there was still no response, she sighed and lowered herself to the grass in despair.

Then a strange thing happened. The cold water dribbled from Black Tip's injured mouth and splashed into the teeth that still gripped bits of his fur. Immediately the body twitched and twitched again. Black Tip jumped back and Vickey sprang to her feet.

'He's alive,' she cried. 'Help him up.'

Black Tip knew better than to go near the other dog fox. The instinct of self preservation was still very strong in him, and he knew how savage a badly wounded fox could be. Realising this, Vickey nosed the now shivering fox over on to his belly and whispered gently in his ear: 'It's all right. Take it easy. We've come to help you.'

Black Tip continued to keep a discreet distance.

'What's your name?' whispered Vickey.

The strange fox snarled. He was groggy and stiff, and as he stirred slowly back to life he felt in no mood to be friendly.

'All right, all right,' said Vickey as soothingly as she could. 'We'll call you Fang because you fought so bravely. Now, Fang, listen to me. We came back to help you. You're badly injured, but I think you're going to be all right. Now try and get back on your feet. We've found a place where you can rest a while.'

Fang got up, fell, got up again, staggered and allowed Vickey to help him up across the slope to the hole in the ice. Black Tip felt it best to stay back for the moment. As with them, the water seemed to revive Fang considerably. By now he realised that on his own, and without cover, he wouldn't make it through the night, so as soon as he felt he could move, he followed the others slowly up the hillside towards the quarry. There, with luck, they could all rest unmolested until they healed.

THREE

Old Sage Brush

A heavy frost set in during the night, and although it would have been a good night for hunting, the three foxes didn't stir. Black Tip's mouth was too sore to catch anything. Vickey's leg had stiffened, and Fang was too weak. At the same time they kept each other warm, and that in itself helped the strength to flow back into their bodies.

Next morning, Vickey reminded Black Tip that they must eat. Not that he needed reminding. He was hungry too. Vickey, however, realised that Black Tip must do the hunting for all of them. Black Tip didn't like the idea very much. While he would forage for her if and when they had cubs, somehow it didn't seem natural that he should do it now, and certainly not for another dog fox.

'It's not natural,' Vickey agreed, 'but it is natural to survive. If you don't bring us food, we'll die. It's up to you now, Black Tip.'

Fang lay with his eyes closed. He would fend for himself when he was well. Anyway, his throat was still too sore even if he did

31

feel like eating. So it was of no interest to him whether Black Tip brought food or not.

Black Tip would have preferred to hunt at night, as he always did, but he knew by the pangs of hunger that he must go now. He stole out of the quarry and sniffed the wind on the high ground. A variety of attractive scents came to his upturned nose and he felt a great temptation to head for the farmyard beyond the meadows. Caution dictated otherwise. He must be careful not to bring any dogs on to his trail, as Vickey and Fang wouldn't be able to out-run them. The shooters hadn't arrived in the meadows yet, so he'd go down there and see what he could find.

The rooks were swirling around the line of tall beech trees away to his right. Their incessant cawing came to him clearly in the cold morning air as he made his way down the frosted fields. The rushes were short and sparse in the meadows and didn't offer much cover. He moved swiftly, yet not even the crumpled brown leaves of the spiky sorrel plants rustled to betray his presence. Here and there he rooted out a few slugs and worms, and over by a frozen stream he pounced on two frogs. This soft food, he found, didn't hurt his mouth. Beneath a hedge he discovered a rabbit burrow and knew by the scent and the droppings that it was occupied.

This surprised him. As a cub, he had been weaned on rabbit food, and later his father had shown him how to hunt rabbits. Then the sleeping sickness had come and the rabbits had disappeared from the hedgerows. Now they were back in this hedgerow at least, and as he waited for them to come out to feed, he relished the thought of something that was almost as tasty as a chicken.

A short wait provided Black Tip with two young rabbits – one he pounced on, and one that ran away from the burrow by mistake. The second one he carried back to the quarry, using a roundabout way to make detection by dogs as difficult as possible. Vickey was delighted and enjoyed it immensely. Fang refused to eat. Not only had his throat been hurt; his pride had been deeply wounded too. Vickey limped a short distance out for a quiet word with Black Tip.

'Fang's feeling very sorry for himself,' she whispered. 'He said nothing at all when you were away. Why don't you get something soft he can eat, maybe a frog or two, and I'll try and talk to him.'

'All right, if you say so.' Black Tip almost felt like saying, 'You wouldn't like me to eat it for him as well?' but felt that would be unkind, so he slipped quietly away.

'Fang,' said Vickey when she returned to the den.

There was no response.

'Fang, you really must snap out of it you know.' There was still no reply, and she went on: 'What happened, happened. You must forget it.'

Fang shifted slightly as if to say he didn't want to talk about it.

'I know your feelings must be hurt,' she continued. 'I'd feel the same if I was in your position. But Black Tip's younger than you are. You can't go on winning forever, you know.'

Fang lifted his head and croaked indignantly: 'What do you mean, younger? I'm only three, you know. Anyway he only won because I slipped. Next time will be different, you'll see.'

Vickey could see that Fang was sensitive about his age. If he said he was three, that meant he was four, and she knew that nowadays few foxes survived to live beyond the age of four.

'There isn't going to be a next time,' she told him firmly. 'I told Black Tip and I'm telling you. If we don't stick together, we'll all die. It's bad enough that man should be killing so many of us, without us killing each other. That's why we went back for you.'

Just then Black Tip returned with two large frogs and dropped them in front of Fang.

'Go on, eat them,' urged Vickey. 'You need to get your strength back as quickly as you can.'

Fang chewed part of a frog and swallowed it with difficulty. The others could see it was painful, and Black Tip felt sorry for him, if not wholly responsible. 'How's your throat?' he asked, trying not to show too much concern.

'It'll be all right,' said Fang hoarsely.

'I only won, you know, because you slipped,' said Black Tip.

'I know,' replied Fang.

Vickey looked at Black Tip as if seeing him in a new light. She was pleased that he had been so generous to Fang. However, she just said: 'It doesn't matter who won. The important thing is that you're both alive.'

'Why?' grunted Fang.

'Because man is getting the better of us,' replied Vickey.

'We know that,' said Black Tip, 'but what can we do about it?'

'We can learn how to survive, said Vickey.

'There's only one way foxes can survive,' croaked Fang, 'and that's to fight.'

'But not each other,' argued Vickey. 'Man is our enemy, and we're losing that fight. We just can't win against him any more – we've forgotten how, even here.'

'What do you mean, even here?' asked Black Tip.

'Because this is the Land of Sinna,' Vickey replied.

Fang grunted in a way that showed quite

clearly he didn't know what she was talking about, and whatever it was, it was nonsense.

Black Tip, however, asked her to tell them more.

'Well, legend has it,' said Vickey, 'that when the fox has been driven from the rest of the country, this is where we'll survive.'

Fang gave another disbelieving grunt, while Black Tip asked: 'Who told you that?'

'A wise old fox.'

'Who was he?'

'An old friend of mine, called Sage Brush. His name means Wise Fox.'

'I know what it means,' said Black Tip a little irritably. He didn't like anyone talking down to him, especially a vixen.

Sensing the reason for his tetchiness, Vickey continued: 'Why do you want to know?'

Black Tip shrugged.

'It must be nice all the same,' Vickey went on.

'What must?' asked Black Tip.

'To know how to survive ... to be able to live without fear of shooters and choking hedge-traps. Not to have to run from the howling dogs, or watch your cubs die before they've really lived...'

Even Fang found the prospect pleasing, adding in his own mind, 'and not to have to fight for a mate!'

'But what was Old Sage Brush trying to

36

say?' wondered Black Tip. 'That this valley contains the secret of survival? That's hard to believe.'

'It sounds a bit far-fetched to me too,' growled Fang.

Slight though it was, Vickey was glad to see the first note of agreement between the two dog foxes.

'There's one way we can find out,' she said.

'How?' asked Black Tip.

'Talk to Old Sage Brush.'

'What for?' asked Fang. 'It's only a waste of time.'

'Why not?' said Black Tip. 'What else have we got to do? You two will be laid up here for a while, and a story from someone like Old Sage Brush would give you something to think about at night when you can't go out to hunt.'

'Good idea,' said Vickey, who had been hoping Black Tip would suggest this all along.

'But is he in this area?' wondered Black Tip.

'It was near here that I met him not too long ago,' said Vickey. 'Anyway, if you circle around you should be able to make contact with him.'

'Right,' said Black Tip. 'I'll do it at gloom-glow.'

The shooters were out again that day, although not in the same numbers as before. It was coming towards the end of the shooting season now, and the game had been severely thinned out. There were only a few old cock pheasants left, and they were too wily to be found. Snipe had moved elsewhere and woodcock were becoming rare. There was no let-up in the winter, and it was too cold to sit in an icy ditch and wait for ducks that might never come.

So it was that when Black Tip set out at dusk he found the meadows empty and no shooters crouching along the thickets beside the streams. Old Sage Brush could wait. First he would eat. From his hiding place in the undergrowth below a holly tree, he scanned the darkening sky. All the clouds had gone and the blue seemed to have frozen into a darker purple. The rich green holly leaves would give him cover that the bare hawthorn hedges wouldn't. He was in the rushiest part of the meadows, having reasoned that if ducks would come down anywhere, it wouldn't be on the frozen stream, but here among the rushes where they could break the ice and poke around for slugs and worms.

Before long a flock of teal flashed overhead with a grace and speed Black Tip admired. They circled high and wide, and landed in the rushes some distance away. He lay still. They were a small duck and had as much meat on their bones as a snipe. With luck a big mallard might see them and think the way was clear to come down. The thought was still going through his mind when two mallard appeared overhead and came in to land about mid-way between himself and the teal. He waited patiently to see what they would do.

Fortunately, the mallard moved away from the teal and came towards the holly tree. They were searching for food beneath the rushes, and he could hear them slipping awkwardly on the ice as they moved closer to him. Now he could see the yellow beak and bottle-green head of the drake, and the brown head of the duck just beyond. A few steps more and the drake was within range. Black Tip sprang and snapped, catching the drake just above the white ring on its neck. The duck took off with a loud flapping and quacking that also sent the teal shooting away into the sky but Black Tip was too busy to notice. He carried the limp body of the drake back to the holly tree, dropped it into the undergrowth where he had been lying, and nudged wisps of withered grass across it. He had a long way to go, and he would collect it on the way back.

That night Black Tip moved in a wide circle. He covered many miles, and on stones and in certain secret places known only to foxes, he left a trail of scents for Old

Sage Brush. At each stop he also raised his head and barked the names of Old Sage Brush and Vickey on the wind. He knew that if the old fox didn't hear him, some other fox would pass the message on. One way or the other, he hoped Old Sage Brush would get to know that Vickey wanted to see him and that he would follow the scent to the quarry at Beech Paw.

Having completed his circle, Black Tip collected the dead mallard and taking care to lift it in such a way that it didn't hurt his sore lip, he carried it back to the quarry. By this time the frost had settled as white as mistletoe on the darkened countryside and he himself looked distinctly white when he arrived at the den. He was glad he had done his hunting first, as he was now tired and cold, and like Vickey and Fang, very hungry.

When Old Sage Brush learned that Vickey wanted to see him, it occurred to him that a younger dog might well have mistaken it for an invitation to a romantic meeting. He smiled at the thought. It flattered him. However, he knew he was too old for that and anyway he realised she already had company. He remembered Vickey well, as he had formed a father-like affection for her. 'If ever I can help you,' he had told her, 'just let me know.' Now she had and now he would.

It was about two nights later that a strange face peeped over the edge of the quarry, and when the way was clear, came down to the den beneath the overhanging rock. None of the three foxes curled up under the rocks knew a thing until the same face peered in at them. Black Tip whipped around with a snarl, but Vickey was at his side in an instant. 'Wait,' she cried, 'it's Old Sage Brush. Sage Brush, is that really you?'

'Who else?' said the stranger. 'Am I not welcome here? I thought I had an invitation.'

'Of course you have,' said Vickey. 'This is Black Tip and Fang. Fang and I are injured. Black Tip is looking after us.'

'You gave us a fright creeping up on us like that,' said Black Tip.

'How else should I tread, but carefully,' smiled Old Sage Brush. 'If the great oak bends before the wind, who am I to raise my head?'

Resent as they might the way the old fox had been able to creep up on them, Black Tip and Fang knew full well that in his own strange way he was telling them it was only because he took extreme care that he had lived so long. And it was only now as he stood at the entrance to their den that they noticed how old he was. His cheek ruffs and whiskers were grey and beard-like, and the scars on his face seemed to underline his years of experience. Snowflakes clinging to his coat cloaked him in a mantle of white in a way that somehow seemed appropriate to his age. It was as they thought of this and looked past him, that the others noticed skiffs of snow swirling around the quarry in the early dawn.

Old Sage Brush sniffed at the remains of the duck, and eased his weary old body down on to the warm earth of the den. Vickey got up and approached him. Her hind leg gave way under her, and she dropped to the ground with a yelp of pain.

'Now, Vickey,' he said, 'how did you get yourself into this mess? And Fang, what happened your throat? You sound hoarse.'

Bit by bit they told the old fox how they had come to be injured, and when they had finished, he said to Vickey: 'You want to be more careful. You had no business being in the meadows at that time. And as for you two, you should be ashamed of yourselves, trying to kill each other.' He stopped and smiled to himself. 'Hmmm, I suppose I did the same myself when I was young, and she is worth fighting over. But she's right, you know. Times have changed. We've got to stick together now. It's them or us.'

'That's what we wanted to talk to you about,' said Vickey. 'That and the legend of Sinna.'

'All in good time,' replied Old Sage Brush. 'First we must eat. Black Tip, it's up to you again I'm afraid. My old bones are too tired, but if you forage around for something, I'll try and get these other two back on their feet. I tell you what, the farm dogs haven't the guts to go out far in the snow. Take yourself off down to the meadow at the end of the farm. The farm ducks only lay in the morning and you can bring back a few eggs. Don't touch the ducks themselves. They'll kick up too much of a fuss and bring the farmer on to us. Hurry now and make the best of the snow. As long as it's falling it'll cover your tracks.'

It was news to Black Tip that farmyard ducks only laid in the morning. Yet the old fox seemed to know what he was talking about. So off he went, keeping to whatever cover he could find to avoid being seen against the snow.

When Black Tip had gone, Old Sage Brush turned to the others. 'Vickey,' he said, 'you must exercise that leg. Otherwise it'll stiffen up completely and you'll never get it back to normal, and a stiff leg is no use to you if you're running for your life. Now's an ideal time to get out and stretch it. And Fang, the air's clear and pure now that the snow has come. It'll do your throat good to get out for a while. You needn't go far, and the snow will soon cover your tracks. Off you go both of you, while I rest up for a bit.'

As Fang and Vickey limped painfully up out of the quarry, Old Sage Brush called after them: 'One more thing. If you meet Black Tip, don't be eating anything out there. Bring it back here where it won't be seen.'

Black Tip was agreeably surprised to find that the ducks had laid their eggs in the meadow, just as Old Sage Brush had said they would, and with the snow reducing visibility and quickly covering his tracks, he made several trips. On his last trip, he caught up with Vickey and Fang returning to the quarry. He was delighted to see how much good the exercise had done them. So was Old Sage Brush, and he told them they must exercise from now on until they were strong enough to fend for themselves again.

The old fox flicked his tongue around his mouth to lick off the remains of an egg yolk. 'Now, Vickey,' he said, 'what's all this about?'

Vickey looked at Black Tip, then at Fang. Whatever about Black Tip, she knew Fang was sceptical about the whole thing. However, she plucked up courage and raised her fine muzzle in a way that said: 'You can think what you like, but I'm going to say it.'

'Well?' urged Old Sage Brush.

'We're fed up with the way we're being treated,' said Vickey. 'We want to learn the secret of survival.'

FOUR

Under Beech Paw

There was something odd about Old Sage Brush that neither Black Tip nor Fang could quite figure out. Perhaps it was his strange habit of never looking them straight in the eye. Whenever he was talking to them, he seemed to look up at the rim of the quarry, or beyond it to the sky, as if it was from some great unseen power out there that he drew his wisdom. When Vickey told him what they wanted, they thought he would burst out laughing. Instead, he just gnawed at a mallard bone and said nothing.

'Vickey said you told her the secret of survival is to be found in this Valley,' ventured Black Tip. 'Can that be so?'

Old Sage Brush looked skywards again, as if making up his mind whether he should take them into his confidence or not. Then he nodded, saying: 'Perhaps.'

'And those who find it?' wondered Vickey. 'Will they learn how to live in peace with man?'

Before the old fox could answer, Black Tip said: 'I was always led to believe we will only find that sort of peace in the after-life.'

'We've all been led to believe that we'll find a happy hunting-ground in the after-life,' said Old Sage Brush.

Fang raised his head as if about to say something, but decided against it.

'I'm sure Fang was taught to believe in the after-life too,' continued Old Sage Brush, 'even though he's an unbeliever now...'

Fang raised his head again, surprised that the old fox should have correctly guessed the reason for his silence, and mumbled something in agreement.

'You see,' said the old fox, 'all creatures have been taught to believe that something better awaits them when they die. Who knows, maybe even man believes the same, although how he feels he deserves it, is beyond me.'

'But the secret of survival,' urged Vickey. 'What do you know about it?'

'I know such a secret does exist for those who wish to seek it,' he told her. 'It doesn't enable them to live in peace with man, but it does enable them to live.'

'And it's to be found here in this valley?' asked Fang, curiosity finally getting the better of him.

Old Sage Brush nodded. 'You see, Vulpes, being the fox god, and therefore being wiser than any of the other gods, did something special for the fox.'

'What was that?' asked Black Tip.

'He realised that the time might come when, like the wolf, foxes might be in danger of being wiped out. So he created a valley where they could learn the secret of survival and so live to perpetuate the species.'

'Do you think the time has come for us to learn that secret?' asked Fang.

'Perhaps,' replied the old fox.

'And perhaps you are the one who can show it to us,' suggested Black Tip.

Old Sage Brush shook his head. 'Alas, I cannot help you.'

'Why not?' asked Black Tip. 'You may be old, but you are very wise.'

'You don't understand,' said Vickey. 'Old Sage Brush can't show us the secret of survival or anything else. I thought you knew. He's blind.'

Black Tip and Fang were flabbergasted. They knew there was something odd about the old fox, but how could he be blind? He had arrived on his own, and with such skill that he had taken them unawares.

'Vickey's right, said Old Sage Brush. 'I lost my eyes a long time ago. Man got fun out of it. I got everlasting darkness.'

'But how did you survive?' asked Fang in a mixture of pity and admiration.

'Fortunately the great god Vulpes endowed us with a sense of smell and hearing that few other creatures can surpass and man cannot match. Strange as it may seem, the loss of my eyes seemed to sharpen my senses, and my wits.' He rested his head again and sighed.

'Sage Brush,' said Black Tip rising to his feet. 'You can still show us the secret of survival.'

'How?' asked the old fox. 'Even if I wasn't blind, I'm too old.'

'Let me be your eyes,' said Black Tip, coming forward.

'And me your strength,' said Fang, joining him.

The old fox thought for a moment. 'And Vickey, what about you?'

Vickey smiled. 'What can I be?'

'Perhaps,' said Old Sage Brush, 'you can be my inspiration.'

'Of course I will,' cried Vickey, her soft amber eyes sparkling with delight. 'Of course I will. Does that mean you'll help us?'

The old fox stroked his whiskers with the back of his right forepaw, and replied: 'After such an offer, how can I refuse?'

'But will we have to leave Beech Paw?' asked Vickey, suddenly having second thoughts. 'Beech Paw is my home. This is where my cubs are – those that have survived.'

'No longer than we do on hunting trips, he assured her. 'Don't forget, Beech Paw is my home too.'

It was agreed that there was no time to lose. Old Sage Brush suggested that they should take any other foxes that wanted to come, and pointed out that they would have to learn the secret of survival by the time the yellow flowers were on the gorse. The old fox was merely expressing an instinct, and yet the others knew exactly what he meant. They'd have to do it well before Vickey's cubbing time.

'But how will we get other foxes to join us?' asked Fang.

'A meeting,' suggested Black Tip.

'Yes, there'll have to be a meeting,' said Old Sage Brush. 'I tell you what we'll do. Black Tip, you go out again. Do a wide circle, inviting other foxes to an important meeting under Beech Paw at the wide eye of gloomglow. Ask them to do likewise, then we'll see how many turn up and if they want to come with us. Off you go now, and take care.'

In the days that followed, Vickey and Fang, acting on the old fox's advice, took as much exercise as they could without going too far from the quarry, so that they might recover fully and build up their strength for whatever lay ahead. Black Tip kept them all well supplied with food, and Old Sage Brush in his own cunning way, soon had him wrestling with Fang. While it was supposed to help Fang exercise, Vickey could see there was more to it than that. Often Fang would get the better of Black Tip, and the whole thing helped to heal not only his broken body, but his injured pride, and by the time it came for the meeting under Beech Paw, the two had formed a firm friendship. Vickey had no doubt that this was exactly what Old Sage Brush wanted.

Beech Paw was a well-known meeting place for foxes. It consisted of a circle of five large beeches, and was called Beech Paw because that was where many a fox's pawprint was to be found. Sometimes a dog fox would slip off for a secret appointment with a vixen there. Or if a dispute arose over territory, that's where it would be settled. It was situated at the upper end of the long row of beeches, the end farthest away from the farmsteads.

When the moon had taken on a fullness that foxes know as the wide eye of gloomglow because it is round and resembles the colour of their own eyes, Black Tip led his three companions to Beech Paw, and there in the hollow between the trees they waited to see who would answer their call.

It was a strange sight, four adult foxes sitting together in a circle of beeches by moonlight, and for a while it seemed their wait was to be in vain. January was just gone, but the biting wind of winter was far from spent as it whistled through the trees and seared across the frosted fields. Above the heads of the waiting foxes, brown crinkled beech leaves clung stubbornly to the nodding branches, defying all efforts of the wind to dislodge them and rustling a brittle refrain. Among the leaves, and almost as numerous as the stars, the husks that held last year's beech-mast gaped open to the sky.

Fang was about to say something, when a pair of eyes peered over the rim of earth that had formed between the trees. Then there were other eyes, and others, and cautiously, one by one, a dozen foxes stole silently into the circle.

Having introduced themselves, Old Sage Brush told the new arrivals of his concern for the way the fox was being slowly extermin-ated, and he asked for a report from them on the situation in their areas. Foxes, of course, don't know counties the way man knows them. Nevertheless, they were able to tell Old Sage Brush that in the Land of the Horse where there was little cover and less food, things were bad, and in Cow Pasture and Crop Land they weren't much better. Even in Heather Plains, Sheep Lands and High Ground, they were coming under increasing pressure, and in Wood Land and Lake Land where they might have been expected to fare better, all creatures were being made

51

welcome, except the fox.

'Just as I thought,' said Old Sage Brush when they had finished. 'Well, that's why we've asked you to come here. We feel the time has come when we must learn the secret of survival.'

Several foxes lowered their heads and sniggered. Having been so sceptical themselves, it was no surprise to Black Tip or Fang that what the old fox had said should be greeted with less than enthusiasm. On the edge of the circle, there was a stealthy movement in the shadows as two or three foxes who considered they were wasting their time, slipped away. Some others clearly thought the whole thing was a joke, and felt they might have a good laugh if they stayed. A few listened and said nothing as if they were prepared to hear Old Sage Brush out before making up their minds one way or the other.

Old Sage Brush answered much the same questions that Black Tip and Fang had asked him, and he explained as he had done to them, how the great god Vulpes in his cunning, had provided for just such a situation as foxes now found themselves in.

'I too have heard of this story,' said one fox. 'But I was told that the secret is known only to the Great White Fox.'

'It is true,' answered Old Sage Brush. 'Foxlore does speak of a great white fox. But it also speaks of courage.'

There was silence, then another fox asked: 'What more can you tell us about this legend?'

Old Sage Brush sat back, and raising his greying head to the wind replied: 'It was with the wind that Vulpes created this Land of Sinna for us – the very same wind you hear in the trees above us.' He eased himself down and continued: 'It was a long long time ago. Vulpes realised that some day his species would face extinction. So he caused a great wind to blow, a wind greater than anything you could possibly imagine. It tore up the trees and ripped open the land and it took the mountains and reshaped them to form the Land of Sinna. He put a great white fox to rule over it, and he called him Sionnach, and he entrusted him with the secret of survival.'

'But that was a long time ago,' said a young vixen. 'Who knows the secret now? And how will we know where to find it? We cannot hear it. We cannot smell it.'

'There is only one way we can find it – and find our way back to Beech Paw,' the old fox replied, and looking at the night sky, told them: 'We must follow the brush.'

Now, man, when he looks at the stars, sees the one thing that perhaps more than any other has helped to shape his destiny. That is the instrument that has spanned two cultures and transformed him from a hunter to a farmer. It is only natural, therefore, when he turns to the stars for guidance, he says, follow the plough. In the same way, when black people escaped from their slavery in the southern states of America and looked north to freedom, they saw in the stars the single most important thing to them – the ladle that gave them food. So they said, follow the ladle. However, when foxes look at the same stars, they don't see a plough or a ladle. Instead, they see the form of a running fox, with the last three stars forming a magnificent tail. And so on winter nights a wise fox will say, follow the brush.

Those assembled under Beech Paw had never before heard such wisdom, and it is no exaggeration to say that at this stage they were overawed by what the old fox had said. Then one fox who knew something the other foxes didn't know, spoke up and asked: 'But who is to show us this secret, old fox? Surely you don't suggest one who is blind?'

At this news there was an uncomfortable murmur among the other foxes.

'It is true,' said Old Sage Brush getting to his feet. 'I am blind.'

Some of the foxes on the fringe rose to their feet, looked at each other and shook their heads as if to say: 'Oh, we might have known there was some catch in it,' or 'So we're supposed to follow a blind fox?' They reckoned they had heard enough, and turned tail and disappeared over the rim of the circle.

'Let them go,' said Old Sage Brush, sensing their departure. 'The loss is theirs. Their eyes may be open, but it is they who are blind. Now who is left?'

'But not only are you blind,' said another fox. 'You are old and weak.'

'It's true,' said Old Sage Brush. 'I am also old, and I do not have the strength of a younger fox. But then it's not only a question of strength. If it was, a bull could catch a hare.'

Despite the obvious wisdom of what the old fox was saying, this fox too turned to go, telling him: 'Sorry Sage Brush, but I think I'll take my chances in Wood Land.' Then another rose and said: 'I'd like to join you, old fox, but my mate is back in Lake Land. My place is with her.'

'Anyone else?' asked Old Sage Brush.

A third fox got up and came forward, saying: 'I'll come.'

The old fox cocked his ear: 'Why do you limp?'

'He's only got three paws,' Black Tip whispered.

'That's right,' said the other fox. 'My right foot got caught in a trap. I had to chew it off

55

to escape. But if you think I'll slow you down...'

'No, no,' said Old Sage Brush. 'That's the sort of courage we need. What name are you known by?'

'Everyone calls me Hop-along.'

'Okay then, Hop-along it is.'

'I'd like to come too,' said a dark-haired vixen. 'My name's She-la.'

'Are you in cub?' asked the old fox.

'No, I have not yet taken a mate.'

'Then you will have time She-la, and you are most welcome.'

'Just two,' whispered Fang to Vickey, 'and one of them has only three legs.'

'Don't be disappointed,' said Old Sage Brush whose acute sense of hearing had picked up what Fang had said. He trotted over the rim of the circle. 'And anyway, it's three if I'm not mistaken.'

Looking over, the others caught a glimpse of a pair of eyes peeping from behind one of the beech trees.

'Skulking Dog,' said Old Sage Brush. 'Why do you hide?'

The fox came out from behind the tree and approached the edge of the hollow cautiously, but didn't answer. It was obvious he was very much a loner and was un-decided whether to join them.

'Well,' said Old Sage Brush, 'it is up to yourself. We're off now. We've little time and a lot to learn. Lead on Black Tip. Don't forget, follow the brush. And if danger threatens, run with the wind – that way, we'll leave less scent.'

FIVE

The Little Brown Hen

As the foxes made their way northwards
along the valley, they were relieved to find
that the shooting had stopped. They had no
way of knowing that the shooting season
had come to an end. All they knew was that
they could now move through the meadows
without fear of being shot, and for that they
were grateful. Other dangers remained, and
sometimes seemed to multiply. The choking
hedge-traps were everywhere and slowed
down their progress considerably. There was
no let-up in the weather either. The nights
were cold, the ground was frozen hard, and
food was difficult to find.

Moving in a group didn't come easily to
them, for it is a fox's nature to live and hunt
alone except at breeding time. This new way
of life presented new problems. A stronger
scent meant a clearer path for dogs to
follow. Above all, it meant more food to be
found, thus increasing the risk of discovery.
Had it not been for Old Sage Brush they
wouldn't have survived the first few days.

Skulking Dog had lingered behind them,

not catching up, not leaving off, not committing himself until he would see how things worked out. All the time Old Sage Brush was aware of his presence, but counselled the others to ignore him unless any of his indiscretions put the group in danger. Black Tip never left the old fox's side, and Fang was never far behind. In general, Fang had turned out to be a great strength, not only to Old Sage Brush, but to Hop-along and the vixens. Vickey was hoping that he might mate with She-la, but she was not yet ready for a mate, and was as independent as any of the dog foxes. Perhaps this was why Old Sage Brush was in no hurry to force the issue with Skulking Dog. He knew that when the time came for She-la to take a mate Skulking Dog wouldn't be long in coming in to join them. He also knew the problems that could cause, as the other two dogs – Fang and Hop-along – wouldn't like the idea of such an attractive she-fox going to an outsider.

At first the group travelled and hunted by night, but they found that this slowed them down too much. Hunting required a lot of time, depending as it did on opportunity as much as anything else. It was something that couldn't be rushed or confined to a particular part of the night. At the same time it wasn't safe for so many of them to travel by day. Realising this, Old Sage Brush came up with the idea that they would get what food they could during the day and travel by the light of the moon, or as they call it, gloomglow. In between, they would get what sleep they needed.

It was also agreed, after much discussion, that they should try and find their food in the wild, rather than risk bringing farmers' dogs out after them. Not being in on these decisions, however, Skulking Dog was unaware that, except for very special reasons, farmyards were now out of bounds to those who would seek the secret of survival.

Skulking Dog, as the others had rightly guessed that first night under Beech Paw, was indeed a loner, a strong dog fox whose stealth and courage always provided him with plenty. However, he was inclined to rely too much on his physical ability and not enough on the cunning brain that the great god Vulpes had given him. If the others hadn't the courage to take food from the farmyards, he wasn't going to pass them by.

He too was forced to forage by day, otherwise he wouldn't have been able to keep up with the others, and this made his visits to the farms doubly dangerous. Yet he was a good hunter, and escaped attention until one day he had what he thought was the good fortune to find a chicken-run. Everything went well until he pounced on his first chicken. Immediately, the other chickens scattered into flight, banging into the wire and falling and screeching in panic. Seeing so many chickens at his mercy, Skulking Dog threw caution to the wind and in a frenzy of excitement snapped the head off every chicken he could find, before grabbing one and squeezing back out through the wire.

It was only when a hail of lead went whizzing over his head that he found the clamour had brought the farmer running out of the house with his shotgun. Realising his mistake, he fled with lead shot singing through the rushes behind him and the farmer's dogs in hot pursuit. Then he made his second mistake. Instead of taking a wide circle, he ran towards the other foxes. They too were forced to flee, and it was only after many miles of dangerous daylight flight that they managed to shake off their pursuers.

Old Sage Brush was very annoyed, and at gloomglow sent Black Tip and Fang to bring Skulking Dog in.

Whether it was because Skulking Dog realised the error of his ways, or because he'd had such a narrow escape, he now felt there might be safety in numbers after all, and allowed the two dog foxes to take him to Old Sage Brush.

The old fox was blunt. He told Skulking Dog that if he didn't join them, he must leave them. They could no longer tolerate him putting the whole group in danger. If he wanted to see how a chicken farm should be raided, he would show him. Reluctantly, Skulking Dog agreed to join them.

After putting a few more miles between themselves and the farmer's dogs, just to be on the safe side, they came to an area of scrub-covered hills. It was an ideal place for foxes, and they hoped they might come upon a local fox, or maybe even a badger, who could brief them on the area and show them where to get food. As in so many other places, however, the foxes and the badgers had gone. Under the gorse on the side of one hill, they found a deserted badger set and took refuge in its maze of tunnels and chambers. Badgers, they had found, were first–class home-builders, and the set was warm and dry and very clean.

As Skulking Dog curled up in a chamber at the back of the earth and sulked, Old Sage Brush assigned Fang to the chamber nearest the entrance where he could keep guard, while he himself retired to another part of the earth to rest. Vickey could see that the flight from the dogs had been a great ordeal for someone of his age. If she was to be his inspiration, she thought, now was the time. Black Tip had gone up to check with Fang that everything was in order and Hop-along and She-la were dozing. Vickey slipped quietly up to the chamber where the old fox was resting and nudged his cheek.

'Sage Brush,' she whispered. 'Are you all right?'

The old fox nodded. 'Just tired.'

'And just a little bit angry?' asked Vickey soothingly.

'I suppose so.'

'Don't worry,' said Vickey. 'It's over now.'

'But it could have meant death for some of us. It would be different if we were all equal; if we were all strong like Fang and Black Tip...'

'What's that you say about Black Tip?'

'Ah, come in Black Tip,' said Old Sage Brush. 'I was just saying to Vickey, it would be different if we were all young and strong like you, but we're not. I'm old and weak and Hop-along has to make do with three legs. So we must act in such a way that our weaknesses are not exposed to our enemies.'

'What do you suggest?' asked Black Tip.

'Well, Skulking Dog has agreed to give us his company, but not his mind. Inside he's still a lone dog, and so long as he continues to think and act like that we remain in danger.'

'How do we change his mind?' asked Vickey.

'I don't know yet. Somehow we'll have to show him that his ways are the ways of death.'

'But isn't it our nature to hunt alone?' said

Black Tip. 'Perhaps it's just that Skulking Dog doesn't know you as we do...'

'And thinks I'm too old and weak to be his leader?' Old Sage Brush considered that before adding: 'Then Skulking Dog must be shown. As Vulpes in his cunning has said, the ivy plant may be too weak to stand alone, but it can overcome the strongest tree.'

Vickey and Black Tip smiled at each other. It gladdened their hearts to see the strength returning to the old fox, and with it the quaint expression of his wisdom.

Returning from a hunting trip, Black Tip and Fang reported hearing a large gathering of poultry in the area. They also brought back two strange eggs they had found in the ruins of an old house – strange, because no matter how much they tried, they couldn't crush the shells.

None of the others had seen eggs like them before. They were the same shape as all hen eggs, maybe a bit shinier, and there was a small hole in each. Perhaps, She-la suggested, something had sucked the yolks out. Could be, they thought, but why then were the shells so hard?

Old Sage Brush, when consulted, couldn't shed much light on the matter, apart from the fact that he recalled having seen eggs like them before. As a young fox, he said, he had found them occasionally in nest boxes, and indeed his cubs had played with them, but he hadn't come across them for a long time now.

While Hop-along and the two vixens amused themselves with the strange eggs, Old Sage Brush put Fang in charge of the earth and went out with Black Tip and Skulking Dog to investigate. He was afraid of what Skulking Dog might get up to in his absence, if he left him behind. He also sensed that perhaps an opportunity was about to present itself to teach him a lesson. Not far from the earth, the sound of many hens brought them to a halt.

'It's coming from the other side of that hill,' said Black Tip.

'Okay, lead on,' said Old Sage Brush, 'and Skulking Dog keep close behind. Don't do anything until I tell you to.'

At the top of the hill there was a gap in the gorse, and there they concealed themselves among the fronds of withered bracken.

'Tell me what you see Black Tip,' whispered Old Sage Brush.

'Down in the hollow, there are three long sheds, and outside two of them is a big funnel. In the first one, that's the one without a funnel, I can see rows and rows of eggs, and new born chicks.'

'What can you see in the next one?'

A workman opened the door of the shed long enough for Black Tip to get a look at the inside.

'I see many wire cages, and each cage seems to be filled with four or five hens.'

'And the next one?'

'I can't see into it at the moment. But wait...'

Several men came around the corner carrying empty buckets, opened the door and went in. Black Tip could see that inside the shed many white hens scratched and cackled, but although the door was partly open, they made no attempt to come out. A few minutes later the men emerged with the buckets full of eggs and closed the door behind them.

'What else do you see?'

'Nothing else?

'Now Skulking Dog,' said Old Sage Brush, 'look around and tell me what you see.'

'Hills,' said Skulking Dog. 'Plenty of cover...' He made to get up.

'Lie down,' ordered Old Sage Brush. 'Just tell me what you see.'

'A little brown hen,' said Skulking Dog, quivering with excitement. 'She's scratching among the gorse on the other hill over there.'

'Now,' said the old fox, 'what would you do if you were to fill your belly?'

'Take the little brown hen.'

'And what about the other hens?'

Skulking Dog was about to say he could

maybe nip in and get one, when he remembered what had happened the last time he had tried something like that.

'Even if you were able to snatch one,' said Old Sage Brush, reading his mind, 'you would only get enough for yourself. What would you do Black Tip?'

'I don't know. I'd have to think about it.'

'Exactly. Well, you stay here Black Tip and observe everything that happens. We'll go back to the earth and tell the others what we've seen, and we'll all think about it.'

While Black Tip settled down to watch the hatchery – and the little brown hen – Skulking Dog led Old Sage Brush back to the earth. The others were still playing with the shiny eggs when they arrived.

'What we have to figure out,' Old Sage Brush told them, 'is how to get enough hens out of there to feed all of us, without drawing man down upon us.'

'It's not possible,' said Skulking Dog. 'If it was, why have other foxes not done it? They've all moved on because they knew there was no point in staying.'

'Let's all think about it and see what we can come up with,' said Old Sage Brush. 'Skulking Dog, you talk it over with Hop-along and She-la. Vickey, maybe you would like to go over and keep Black Tip company, and if you see anything worthwhile, come back and tell me. This requires much thought.'

Old Sage Brush retired to his chamber. Maybe, he thought, they should be getting back to Beech Paw. At the same time, maybe he was being given this opportunity to demonstrate to Skulking Dog that the great god Vulpes had provided him with more between his ears than a mouthful of teeth. Most certainly it would save time in the long run if Skulking Dog could be brought into line now.

The old fox thought long and hard, yet it wasn't until Vickey returned to report that the little brown hen had visited her nest but hadn't settled, that he got an idea.

'Vickey,' he said, 'you are indeed my inspiration. Fetch Black Tip.'

Old Sage Brush gathered his little group around him, and told them that with the aid of Vulpes – and Vickey – he had hit upon a plan. He didn't tell them exactly what it was, just enough to set it in motion, as he wanted it to have the maximum effect on Skulking Dog.

'Black Tip,' he said, 'you and Skulking Dog take these shiny eggs up to the hill and leave them in the coldest, frostiest place you can find. After a while, steal up to the hill again, to the nest of the little brown hen.' He thought for a moment. He had no way of knowing that hens, unlike foxes, have very little sense of smell. However, he did know that birds could often tell if anything had been at their nest, and he didn't want to arouse the suspicions of the little brown hen, so he told them: 'Take the shiny eggs and put them in the nest. But be careful you don't disturb it. If there are any of her own eggs in it, bring them back. We can have those for a start. Then I'll tell you what to do next.'

Black Tip and Skulking Dog did as they were told.

That evening in the dusk before gloom-glow, Old Sage Brush despatched Fang to the sheds in the hollow, and sent Black Tip and Skulking Dog back up the hill to where the little brown hen had her nest beneath a gorse bush. A hard frost had set in, and a freezing wind was cutting across the hill.

While Fang roamed around the sheds, disturbing the white hens and keeping them awake, Black Tip and Skulking Dog crawled quietly through the undergrowth until they were near the little brown hen. They could see she hadn't settled down for the night. She was still scratching about, complaining to herself about the hard ground and the frost. When at last she did settle into the nest, she felt what she thought were her eggs, as cold as two lumps of ice. Jumping up with a loud cackle, she walked around for a few moments before returning to the nest and flicking them out with her beak.

Old Sage Brush had predicted that the

coldness of the eggs would start the little brown hen thinking about the warm sheds in the hollow. Even if it did, they had no idea what purpose it would serve. The old fox hadn't told them. The little brown hen shifted uncomfortably in her nest. It had been a very hard winter on the hill. Never before had she known it to be so cold. She had hoped to have a brood of chicks to keep her company. Sadly, none of her eggs had hatched and it seemed her latest ones had turned to stone. She got out of her nest and pecked at the two delft eggs the foxes had left in place of her own. They were indeed as hard as stones. To make matters worse, she could now hear for the first time in a long while, the barking of foxes across on the other hill.

In their hiding place nearby, Black Tip and Skulking Dog looked at each other. They knew the barking was more of Old Sage Brush's work.

Settling back into her nest, the little brown hen shivered and wondered what she would do. She could hear the hens cackling away in the sheds in the hollow. She thought how she had often seen the eggs there, and the fluffy little day-old chicks. Through the partly-open door of one shed she had also seen the white hens eating and drinking and sitting in their warm nest boxes. They didn't have to worry about foxes or to scratch and scrape for food the way she had. They had other hens to keep them company, and cockerels too. They had a warm nest at night and their eggs brought forth chickens. Maybe, she thought, it was time to give up this hard and lonely life on the hill. She knew that every day when the men came to visit the shed, they left the door just a little bit open. If she was quick, perhaps she could hop inside and no one would notice.

Next morning, when the men with the buckets went into the third shed, Black Tip and Skulking Dog watched from the bracken. Sure enough, they saw the little brown hen scurrying across to the shed and slipping through the partly-open door.

Old Sage Brush was pleased, and told them that all they had to do now was wait for results. Privately he prayed that his plan would work. Experience had taught him that creatures were never happy with what they had; they always felt that others were better off than they were. In the case of the little brown hen, he believed she would soon realise how well-off she had been on the hill. He only hoped it wouldn't take her too long.

Down in the shed, the little brown hen found herself in more company than she ever dreamed of. There were hundreds of hens and cockerels. There was food and drink any time she wanted it, and warm nest boxes around the walls. She made friends with many other hens, and with a young cockerel. The cockerel was surprised he hadn't noticed her before, and she could see he was attracted to her.

In spite of all this, the novelty of the shed quickly wore off, just as Old Sage Brush thought it would. There was always pushing and shoving to get to the food that was poured into the large funnel and carried along a trough in the shed. Even when she could get at the food, it always tasted the same. While she thought the shed was warm at first, she now found it stuffy and over-crowded. She couldn't sit in the nest box any time she wanted, or even as long as she liked. Others had to use them too. How she longed for her own little nest under the gorse bush and the stars, with the wild wind caressing her soft brown feathers.

Seeing that she was unhappy, some of the other hens, and the young cockerel, asked her what was wrong. Naturally she told them of her life on the hill, where she was free to come and go as she pleased, eat what food she liked, and had a nest of her own. Of course, this was all new to the others, who were aware of no other world outside the shed where they had been reared. The more the little hen talked of the freedom she had enjoyed on the hill, the more the others realised the extent of their enslavement and the more they longed for the other way of life.

How well Old Sage Brush knew his fellow creatures. Some of these birds, who had never even thought of venturing outside the shed before, now wanted to leave with the little brown hen, and that evening, when the men left the door partly open again, that's exactly what they did. Unnoticed, seven or eight of them followed her out and up to the hill. However the little brown hen had only told them of all the good things in the wild, and had forgotten to tell them of its dangers. Consequently, the silly hatchery hens walked not to freedom, but into the jaws of Old Sage Brush and the other foxes. As for the little brown hen, she knew better. She escaped to her old haunts, together with her admiring young cockerel.

So, the little brown hen was happy again – and so also were the occupants of the badger set across on the other hill. The foxes ate their fill and then, turning their backs to the brush, they made their way back home to Beech Paw.

SIX

Hop-along's Dream

There was no gloomglow and no running fox
in the sky. Snow clouds covered the moon
and the stars, and snow swirled around the
fields and farms of Beech Paw. In the quarry
above the meadows, the foxes snuggled down
in the warmth of their earth, and no swirling
snow or freezing winds found their way in.

Old Sage Brush had decided they had
earned a rest. His plan with the little brown
hen had worked out so well that they had
not drawn any danger upon themselves, a
point he was quick to impress upon the
others, especially Skulking Dog. The men at
the hatchery weren't even aware that they
had lost any poultry, so there was no
pursuit. As an added precaution, Old Sage
Brush had also insisted that they follow the
badger's example, and not leave any chicken
remains lying around where the men might
see them.

'That has got more foxes killed than anything else I know,' he said. 'Except, of
course, the choking hedge-traps. You might
as well leave a message on your doorstep

saying Foxes in Residence. It's suicide.'

The others listened attentively. Vickey snuggled in beside Black Tip, and She-la was enjoying the company of Hop-along with whom she had now mated. Fang and Skulking Dog would have to look elsewhere for vixens, but for now they were content to lie and listen to the old fox. The admiration of the little group for Old Sage Brush had grown immeasurably with the success of the hatchery raid. They had never seen anything like it before. To get so many hens out would have been an achievement in itself. To do so without having to go there themselves, or without bringing dogs or shooters after them, was nothing short of genius. It would be told and retold and end up in foxlore, an example to those who had forgotten that the great god Vulpes had endowed them with something special.

'And that,' said the old fox, 'is cunning. You wouldn't think it, to look at the state we're in today, that we're supposed to be cunning. You'd think man is the one who's cunning.'

'He's been cunning enough to destroy many of us,' observed Black Tip.

'Yet,' said Old Sage Brush, 'man speaks of the fox as the cunning one, I believe. I've heard it said that he talks of being "as cute as a fox", or of trying to "out-fox". But are we cute? We're being shot to death and choked by the thousand. I believe man tells his children stories about wolves, then reassures them there is no such thing as a wolf in this country any more. He tells them stories about foxes too. Will he soon be assuring them there is no such thing as a fox?'

'We know what you say is true,' said She-la. 'And we know you have great wisdom. But if one such as you can be blinded by man, what hope is there for the likes of us? How can we hope to survive?'

'You have just got a great lesson in how to use the cunning Vulpes has given you,' replied the old fox, 'and it has been a cheap lesson. I paid dearly for mine.'

'You don't have to tell us about it if you don't want to,' said Black Tip.

'I don't mind. If it was a lesson for me, so too it can be a lesson for you.' Old Sage Brush nestled his grey head between his forefeet. 'It happened during my last breeding season.' He sighed. 'I can see myself in all of you. I was a young fox then – strong and independent, like you Black Tip, ferocious, like you Fang, and foolhardy, like you Skulking Dog.'

Skulking Dog lowered his head, and sensing that he had hurt his feelings, the old fox added quickly: 'Not that I'm saying you're foolhardy now, Skulking Dog. I'm hopeful you've learned your lesson. When I learned mine, I was all of these things, and so I became severely handicapped, like you Hop-along.' As he continued, none of the other dog foxes felt offended by what he had said. Strangely, they felt privileged to be identified with him, if only in a negative way. He went on: 'No badger set or rabbit burrow would do me, and so I had to scrape out my own earth in a sand pit on the side of a hill covered with gorse. An old fox I knew had warned me never to make my home in a sand pit, but I was too proud to take his advice. I found the sand easy to scrape and easy to shape.'

'We had a nice earth,' he recalled, 'and we had a fine litter – three in all, two dogs and a vixen. I loved them with all the love a father can give. They were cuddly and very playful, and if a father can have a favourite, I suppose I must admit it was the little she-fox, Sinnéad. She was born with a small white mark on her forehead and was the cutest little thing you ever saw. But I loved them all and hunted hard to make sure they wanted for nothing.'

He sighed. 'Unfortunately, I went back to the same farm too often. The men came from the farm with their guns and their fun dogs, and long sticks. Unlike the badger, I hadn't thought of putting a back door in my earth. The small fun dogs came right in and cornered us.'

'So that's why you wouldn't let us block

up the back door of the badger set?' said Vickey.

'What did they do with the long sticks?' asked Hop-along.

'I'm afraid they were more cunning than I was,' continued the old fox. 'They sank the long sticks down through the sand to find out where we were. They kept pushing them down, poking and probing. The end of one stick was right at my head. It kept jabbing at my eyes and my face, but I knew if I snapped at it the men would know they had located us. For what seemed an eternity, I endured the jabbing pain, the choking sand and the snapping dogs, until at last little Sinnéad could bear to see me suffer no longer. She sprang from behind me and grabbed the end of the stick. How could she know that was exactly what the men above wanted? It told them where we were and they dug down. My vixen and two dog cubs were shot where they lay. Sinnéad and I made a run for it. The blood was streaming from my eyes, and as I crashed headlong through the under-growth I could just make out one of the men diving after Sinnéad and catching her. It was the last thing I ever saw.'

Old Sage Brush paused and sighed. 'Poor Sinnéad. She'd have been a nice mature vixen now, like you Vickey, or She-la. But it wasn't to be.'

Outside the quarry, the cold wind drove

78

the snow across the hillside. Inside, the younger foxes curled up and went to sleep, secure in the earth and in the company of one who had learned so much the hard way.

In the days and nights that followed, the weather showed a slight improvement, and once again they made their way northward along the valley. The younger foxes were learning much from Old Sage Brush. At the same time, Vickey let it be known that he felt perhaps they were beginning to rely too heavily upon his cunning and experience, and that he wished to find out just how much they had learned.

Several times Vickey and the others asked Old Sage Brush about Sionnach, the Great White Fox he had spoken of back at Beech Paw. However, it was a subject on which he would not be drawn further. 'Some things I can show you – others you must see for yourselves,' was his reply, and no matter how many times they asked him, that was all he would say.

The days were getting a little longer now, and occasionally the sun would appear for short periods. It gave a new life to the air, although there were few signs that it was finding its way down into the soil. Only bunches of cow parsley braved the cold to give the barren ditches a new mantle of green and a suggestion of spring. Otherwise the winter lingered on. Fortunately, the frosty nights also gave the foxes a clear view of the running fox in the sky, and so long as they could see the brush they knew which direction they were going.

It was in a most unexpected way that they were brought to a halt. They had found a stream where they could refresh themselves and rest before continuing their nocturnal travels. There were no dogs to be heard, nor was man to be seen, although his traces were clearly apparent. Pieces of plastic fertiliser bag flapped in the hedgerow, and a green bottle lay discarded to litter the stream. It was a slow-moving stream with hardly any banks, which made the water easy to get at. Having slaked their thirst, they took cover beneath the hedge.

Later, as they slept, darkness closed around them and the moon crept across the sky. Whatever about the others, Hop-along began to dream, and it was a dream that reflected a worry that was now beginning to occupy his mind. How was he, a fox with only three legs, going to prove himself to Old Sage Brush? Above him, the moon was big and bright, and smiling, as if it and it alone was sharing the secrets of his slumber. If it was, it saw Hop-along's secret thoughts slipping silently out of the hedgerow, across the stream, and into the fields beyond…

In a way that can only happen in dreams,

Hop-along suddenly found himself with his friends in fairly high country, and it was no surprise to them to come upon a hare sitting in the moonlight. Foxes, of course, will kill a hare if they can, but this one showed no fear of them. Instead he sprang up with a sudden thrust of his hind legs in a spectacular leap across the moon. When he landed, he scudded around and, sitting back on his haunches, bared his buck teeth in a twitching grin. It was clear from his behaviour that he wasn't playing with them. He was inviting them to come and get him.

The foxes, it must be said, had no reason to fear the hare. They knew he could outrun them with those powerful hind legs. Yet if it came to a standing fight, the fox would win. Why then was this hare so brazen as to take on several foxes?

The hare hopped warily around. 'Which one of you calls yourself leader?' he asked in a very lofty manner.

Old Sage Brush stepped forward, and the hare laughed. 'You?' he sneered. 'You call yourself leader? You are too old. There would be no victory in fighting you.'

Hop-along knew that this hurt the old fox's feelings, and the others knew it too, but Sage Brush wasn't prepared to let himself be goaded into a fight he couldn't win, so he said: 'Then, let me name one who will take up your challenge on my behalf.'

'By all means,' sneered the hare. 'If you can find one strong enough.' So saying, he gave another impressive leap across the sky.

'Fang is my strength,' said Old Sage Brush. 'But our weakest is strong enough to put you in your place, you over-grown rabbit.'

'Ho-ho,' laughed the hare in mock glee. 'An overgrown rabbit am I? We'll soon see about that.' Thereupon he made a fierce warning sound by grinding his teeth. They could hear the sound being picked up and relayed by other hares across the hills, and in what appeared to be no time at all, hundreds of hares had bounded over the stone walls and gathered around in a huge circle to watch them.

'They say I'm just an over-grown rabbit,' announced the big hare who had called them. The other hares ground their teeth and grinned widely at the idea. 'Me, Lepus, Leader of Hares, an overgrown rabbit,' he continued. He gave several more long leaps, then turning again to his fellow hares, appealed to them, saying: 'What will we do with them?'

'Kill them!' cried the other hares. 'Kill them!'

Lepus bade them be quiet. 'I am not only the leader of the hares. I am a great hare. No, I will not kill them – not yet.'

He turned to the foxes and told them: 'I am Lepus the Great. I can jump higher than any other hare. So here's what I will do. If you can prove yourselves worthy by jumping higher than I can, I will let you go.'

The other hares ground their teeth and grinned and rubbed their front feet together in glee. They knew no other creature could jump as high as Lepus.

Hop-along knew, as all the foxes did, that they could not possibly jump as high as any hare, not to mention Lepus. Even the strongest of them knew it. They turned to Old Sage Brush. The old fox knew it, but he said to Lepus:

'You have laughed at me because I am weak. But there is one of us who is weaker, and it is he who will take up the challenge.' So saying he turned to Hop-along and told him: 'Hop-along, it was you who brought us here, so it is you who must out-jump the hare.'

'What?' exclaimed Lepus indignantly. 'You dare to put up a three-legged fox against Lepus the Great. That would be no contest.'

'Of course, if you are afraid...' replied Old Sage Brush.

'Afraid?' said Lepus. 'I am afraid of no fox, and certainly not one with three legs. Let the contest begin.'

Silence descended on the hillside, and Hop-along's heart sank. The old fox, he realised, was offering him no words of wisdom, no thoughts of cunning, and he'd have to think his way out of this one himself. It was plain they couldn't out-run the hares, and anyway, they were surrounded. And being out-numbered, they couldn't fight. He also knew he couldn't jump half as high as Lepus. So he lay down and put his head on his paw and thought about it.

Maybe, he thought, his hind legs had become stronger than any other fox's because of his handicap. But then, what was it that Old Sage Brush had said back at Beech Paw? He had said it wasn't a question of strength; that if it was, a bull could catch a hare. If that was so, there must be some other way to deal with this hare. But what was it?

As Hop-along lay there and thought about what he was going to do, he glanced up and saw that something seemed to have taken a small bite out of the wide eye of gloomglow. He had no way of knowing that he was now seeing what man calls a partial eclipse. All he knew was that the eye of gloomglow wasn't as round and full as it had been when it had crept into the sky. Then he looked at the big staring eyes of Lepus, and he had an idea. He had noticed that, unlike foxes, hares had their eyes in the sides of their heads, instead of in front. The reason for that, he thought, was probably to enable them to see danger coming from either side, and it occurred to him that if that was so, they might not be able to see forward or upward as well as foxes.

Hoping he was right,. Hop-along waited until the moon had gone behind the clouds. Then he got up and hobbled over to Lepus. 'I accept your challenge,' he told the leader of the hares. 'You jump first so that I may see what I have to beat.'

'Ha!' laughed Lepus. 'And so you shall see.' With that, he gave a mighty leap into the night sky and landed about fifteen feet away. 'Now,' he said proudly, 'beat that.' The watching hares grinned widely and rubbed their forefeet together again.

Hop-along's friends had been listening and watching in silence. They knew well he could not possibly jump as high. At the same time, they realised he must have something in mind, so they stayed silent.

'Well?' taunted Lepus. 'Why don't you jump?'

'In a moment,' said Hop-along, keeping a sly eye on the moon. 'I'm just collecting my strength.' He could see the moon was still behind the clouds. 'True,' he went on, playing for time, 'you have made a great leap, almost as high as the wide eye of gloomglow. But I will do better. I will jump so high that I will take a bite out of the very eye of gloomglow.'

The hares laughed and cocked their heads to one side to try and see the moon. It was just beginning to edge its way from behind the clouds, the shadow of the eclipse still hidden from their view. Hop-along crouched low into a ball, launched himself into the sky with all the strength he could muster, and snapped his teeth with an almighty bark. The moon had now come out from behind the clouds, and even the hares could see that a bite had been taken out of it. Frightened, they cowered back and screamed as if in agony. Hop-along's friends, on the other hand, jumped forward and barked in sheer delight at his success.

True to his word, Lepus silenced the gathering of hares, and said: 'Hop-along, truly you are a great fox. Never before have I seen any living creature do such a thing. You are all free to go now, and in honour of your great achievement, if there is any favour we can bestow upon you, you need only ask.'

Hop-along thanked him, but explained that the greatest gift they could have was their freedom, and now that they had it, they were anxious to move on. Lepus wished them luck, and the gathering of hares sent them on their way with a great cheer.

When they had left the hares and the high country well behind them, the foxes stopped to regain their composure and to rest.

'You have done well, Hop-along,' said Old Sage Brush. 'That was truly a trick worthy of Vulpes himself.'

The others congratulated him too and wanted to know how he did it. What magic had he wrought to take a bite out of the eye of gloomglow? they asked.

'No magic,' replied Hop-along. 'It's thanks to our leader, Old Sage Brush, that I was able to do it. Hasn't he taught us to use our cunning instead of our strength? I realised he knew I could not win by strength. So I did what he told Black Tip and Skulking Dog to do back on the hill. I lay down to see all that I could see, and I knew that I could see more than the hares. Knowing that we had faith in our own survival, the great god Vulpes did the rest...' There the dream faded from Hop-along's mind.

A short time later, on the banks of a slow-moving stream, Hop-along and his fellow-foxes woke up and looked around them. Pieces of plastic fertiliser bag flapped in the hedge nearby, and a discarded green bottle littered the stream.

'What had happened?' he asked himself. Had they really been away in the Land of the Hares? Had he really out-jumped Lepus the Great? Or had it all been a dream? He looked up at the moon, but it only smiled back and told him nothing. Then he looked down at the place where his paw should be, and he knew it had to be a dream. However, he also knew now that he was learning from

Old Sage Brush.

Rising quickly, they crossed the stream and slipped away into the fields beyond.

SEVEN

Prey of the Howling Dogs

The running fox in the sky was now beginning to lean over backwards on its brush. The nights were still frosty, but there was a slight suggestion of warmth in the sun. The farmers had done much of their ploughing, and that was a good thing. It attracted more wildlife into the fields in search of food, and that in turn gave the foxes greater opportunities to hunt. They might well have wondered where all the new birdlife came from as the weather improved, but they didn't. They were just glad to see it.

It was also lambing time on some farms. Stray dogs were savaging ewes, and hooded grey crows were gathering to see if they could pick off any new-born lambs. Whatever temptations Old Sage Brush's group had in that respect, they knew they had to be extremely careful not to bring the wrath of the sheep farmers down on their heads, and so they continued to avoid the farmers as much as possible.

Everywhere rooks were nesting high in the trees and lining the roads in great numbers.

The purpose of their roadside vigil seemed to be the worms that were knocked up to the surface of the grass verges by passing vehicles. Next autumn it would be barley and wheat falling from passing lorries. In the mean time, enough of the rooks were killed on the roads to provide occasional pickings for the foxes. Much more worthwhile were the small birds in the hedgerows. There were also rats and field mice and, occasionally, a hedgehog, to vary the diet, and of course, beetles for dessert!

Skulking Dog lay on his belly and watched a big dung beetle at work in a cake of cow dung. They were resting in the corner of a field, and on the dead branch that lay across a gap in the hedge, Fang could see the squiggly scars he knew to be the work of a bark beetle. Clawing off a piece of bark on top, he was rewarded by the discovery of a squirming patch of larvae, and the vixens gathered round to share it.

Old Sage Brush was worried about Skulking Dog, and he told Black Tip and Vickey about it.

'He's brooding all right,' agreed Black Tip. 'Probably misses his old way of life – and the chicken farms.'

'What do you think, Vickey?' asked the old fox.

'I think what he needs is a nice vixen to look after him.'

'So do I,' said Old Sage Brush. 'Well, we'll see what happens. Maybe we'll find a nice mate for him this time. Meanwhile, Black Tip, keep an eye on him for me in case he gets himself into any more trouble.'

Black Tip undertook to do this, although he soon found it easier said than done. There was much work to do. Fox paths, for example, had to be checked out, especially where they went through road-side hedges. Trappers knew well that foxes were in the habit of using the same places to cross roads, and it had become a favourite trick of theirs to put choking hedge-traps at these particular points. Hunting took up a lot of time too, and they all had to take their turns at it, including Skulking Dog. Even when Black Tip and Skulking Dog went out together, it wasn't always possible to stay together. Old Sage Brush readily accepted this when Skulking Dog got into trouble again. He realised he had been asking Black Tip to do the impossible.

It was a dark night when it happened. Clouds once again obscured gloomglow, and they couldn't follow the brush, but it was a good night for hunting. Scents were strong and it was the turn of Black Tip and Skulking Dog to forage for food. Everything went well until they arrived at an area of scrub-land that clearly held the scent of pheasant. This was a welcome break, because after the shooters had stopped coming to the fields, they had found pheasants very scarce. There was no point in going into the undergrowth together, so they split up and approached it from different directions.

Black Tip was getting the scent of the pheasant very strongly when the call of a strange fox halted him in his tracks. He recognised the love call of a vixen and it had come from away over on the other side of the scrub, somewhere in the direction Skulking Dog had gone. Normally, Black Tip wouldn't have worried. It was the possibility that Skulking Dog might get into a fight with another dog fox that caused him some concern. If he got injured, like Fang, they might have to go on without him.

Skulking Dog had been about to enter the scrub from the far side when the love call of the vixen turned him back. He listened. There it was again. A surge of excitement swept through his body, and throwing caution to the wind, he responded to her call, and set off to pay his respects, the pheasant and all thoughts of food forgotten.

Beyond the scrub was a piece of commonage, and it was from there that the call of the vixen had come. Skulking Dog heard it again. It was nearer this time, and he hurried towards it. So occupied was he with the thought of finding a mate, that he failed to see the shadow of a car parked in off the road. Suddenly a powerful light cut through the night, catching him in its glare. Blinded for a moment, he turned to run. Several explosions shattered the stillness of the night, and a hail of shots ripped into the grass beside him.

As Skulking Dog streaked into the darkness beyond the circle of light, a man shouted: 'Missed it.' They had no way of knowing that they hadn't entirely missed. One of their shots had caught Skulking Dog on the rump, injuring him, not seriously, but enough to cause him severe pain. Moments later, Black Tip was beside him. There was no sign of pursuit, and with Black Tip helping him whenever he could, they returned to where the others were waiting.

Old Sage Brush was annoyed with himself. He had forgotten all about the love calls of death. Imitating the call of a vixen to attract a dog fox was a fairly new trick man had thought up. It struck at the very nature of the fox, preying upon his natural instinct to mate and survive. Obviously Skulking Dog hadn't encountered this trick before, and the least the old fox felt he could have done was to warn him.

'Don't blame yourself,' consoled Black Tip. 'I'm the one to blame.'

'You couldn't help it,' said the old fox. 'What I asked you to do could not be done by any fox.'

'I don't mean that,' said Black Tip. 'You see, I knew of this trick. Not the love call, but something similar. Once I was almost caught the same way, only then man was imitating the squeal of a trapped rabbit. I thought I was going to get an easy meal. Instead, I almost ended up just like Skulking Dog.'

'We're all to blame for not being more careful – me, you, Skulking Dog, all of us. Man may not be a fox, but he has a lot of cunning. We never know what he'll think up next.' The old fox paused. 'Anyway, how is Skulking Dog now?'

Black Tip went over to where Skulking Dog was lying in the bracken. Vickey and She-la were attending to his wounds.

'How is he?' he asked.

'I'm all right,' growled Skulking Dog.

'You'll be all right when I get these pellets out of your back,' said Vickey firmly.

Skulking Dog had taken some gun-shot along the top of the back, and Vickey knew well what he must be suffering. Now she did for Skulking dog what Black Tip had done for her when she had been wounded in the hind leg back in the meadow near Beech Paw. One by one she located the pellets. They were as numerous, she thought, as seeds of goose grass in summer, and clung many times more tightly. Skulking Dog suffered in silence while Vickey patiently got her teeth behind each one and gently eased it out through his torn skin.

'There you are, that's the last of them,' she announced finally. 'A few days rest and you'll be all right.'

Skulking Dog scrambled to his feet. 'There'll be no few days rest for me,' he told her. 'There's nothing wrong with my legs, and the sooner we're on the move again, the better.'

'That's the spirit,' said Old Sage Brush. 'But we still have to eat, and you can rest up until Black Tip and Fang go out and find us some food.'

'Can I go too?' asked She-la.

'Another time,' said the old fox. 'I'd rather you helped Vickey make doubly sure there are no pellets left in Skulking Dog, and clean his wounds thoroughly. We don't want to lose him.'

'Mark my words,' said Vickey. 'What Skulking Dog needs is a nice vixen to look after him. It would make a new fox of him.'

Foxes – male or female – were few and far between. They were now in an area of rich pastures, where cattle grazed and horses neighed and whinnied and galloped around the fields. There were several big houses in the district, and around each sprawled a profusion of undergrowth that promised both cover and food. Rooks were swarming around the tree-tops in their thousands, and wood-pigeons flapped in and out of the trees as they tried to settle on flimsy branches. Down below, leaves of wild arum were sprouting among the dead leaves and withered grass, but it would be a long time yet before their flowers – the lords and ladies of the undergrowth – would venture out.

'Isn't it lovely,' smiled She-la. 'There are beetles beneath the leaves and birds in the bushes.'

Vickey nodded and sniffed. 'And a strong smell of pheasant in the wind. It *is* nice, isn't it?' Everything seemed to be better here than ever she had seen before. The cover was thicker, and the food plentiful. Even the weeds were taller, she thought, gazing up at the towering stalks of giant hogweed, easily twice the size of those she had seen in the hollow the day Black Tip and Fang had fought for her back at Beech Paw.

'You know we can't stay here,' said Old Sage Brush.

The vixens looked at him in surprise, and Skulking Dog who was with the old fox answered their unspoken question, saying: 'Don't you know? This is the Land of the Howling Dogs.'

All foxes had heard of the howling dogs. Even those who hadn't been chased by them had nightmares about them.

'Skulking Dog was reared not far from a

place with howling dogs,' said Old Sage Brush.

'And many a good run I gave them,' said Skulking Dog.

'So did I,' said the old fox. 'But not any more. I'd be an easy catch for them now. So would Hop-along, and I doubt if all the cunning in the world could save us.'

'Then we must move on quickly,' said Vickey. 'Let's tell the others.'

When they joined the others in deeper cover, they found that they already knew about the howling dogs as they had a visitor. He was a local fox who had become aware of their presence and come to warn them of the danger.

'But what is the secret of *your* survival?' asked Vickey. It was a question she had decided to ask every fox she met. 'I mean,' she added, 'if the howling dogs are so dangerous, why have they not caught you?'

'Because,' said the stranger, 'like the great running fox in the sky, I never stop running long enough to give them the chance.'

'Tell me, Running Fox,' said Vickey, who loved putting names on her fellow-creatures, 'when are the howling dogs likely to come again?'

'It's difficult to say. There is a man many fields away. He sets choking hedge-traps, and I know he has a fox in a cage. Soon he will let it out for the howling dogs.'

'Oh, how horrible!' said She-la. 'Will it get away?'

'I doubt it,' said Running Fox. 'It's a stranger in this area and doesn't know the tricks I know. I doubt it.'

Needless to say, no reputable hunt will capture a fox and let it out in strange surroundings for the sake of a chase. In this case, however, one member of the hunt, wishing to impress a visitor, had paid a local trapper to get a fox and let it out in a certain piece of woodland where the hounds would almost certainly come across it.

Old Sage Brush sighed. He hated the thought of leaving another fox to the mercy of the howling dogs.

'Let me have a look,' said Skulking Dog.

Old Sage Brush hesitated.

'I'll show him the way,' offered Running Fox. 'There's an empty badger set in these woods. If you lie low there and take care not to be caught in the open, you should be all right.'

Old Sage Brush agreed and Running Fox led them to a set that was well concealed by the glossy green leaves of a clump of rhododendron bushes. Soon the old fox, Hop-along, She-la and Vickey were curled up in the central chambers, with Black Tip and Fang in chambers that allowed them to guard the entrance and exit.

As darkness fell and gloomglow spread

across the countryside, Running Fox led Skulking Dog into the silent fields, past groups of cattle lying in the grass chewing their cuds, over meadows and through woodland, until they came to a small house at the end of a long lane. From the safety of a high bank at the back, Running Fox showed him a shed and told him: 'The fox is in there. The door is tied with wire, and there are fun dogs in the house. I don't think it would be wise to go any nearer.'

Skulking Dog was thinking hard. He had yet to show Old Sage Brush that he had learned to use his cunning, but think as he would, he couldn't imagine how he might release the fox.

'There's a big house not far from here,' said Running Fox, 'and it has no fun dogs. We can hide there until we decide what to do.' He smiled, and added: 'In the morning I'll introduce you to some other foxes there.'

'Vixens?' asked Skulking Dog hopefully.

Running Fox smiled again. 'You'll be the best judge of that, and if they are you can have one – if you can catch it!'

Skulking Dog was intrigued, but he didn't inquire further about it. He knew Running Fox was teasing him a little bit, and that he wasn't going to learn anything more about it until they were at the big house.

They were going to a house that used to be the mansion of a wealthy estate owner. The estate had long since been taken over by the Land Commission for division among local farmers, and the house itself was being used by the Government as an energy research centre. When the oil-producing countries of the Middle East had pushed up their prices, several projects had been undertaken to explore the possibilities of alternative sources of energy. In the West of Ireland, windmills were spinning merrily before the Atlantic wind, but in other parts of the country scientists were concentrating their efforts on solar energy. It was for this purpose that research workers had moved into the big house. Dogs and cats they considered a nuisance and a waste of time, a fact that local wildlife, like Running Fox, soon came to appreciate.

A short time later, Running Fox and Skulking Dog stole among the outhouses, and after feeding on some of the many mice that had over-run the place, they settled down in the comfort of a burst bale of straw.

'In the morning,' whispered Running Fox, 'I'll show you the other foxes I was telling you about.'

Shortly after dawn, Running Fox took Skulking Dog into the lawns of the old mansion. A weed called winter heliotrope had encircled the lawns with a carpet of broad green leaves. Its flowers had now keeled over, as if the winter had proved too much for them, but their unique fragrance, which once had brought them from Italy to the gardens of Europe's wealthy, still left a scent of almonds in the air.

Nice though this was, Skulking Dog snorted to expel it from his nostrils, for something else had stopped him in his tracks, something he couldn't smell and couldn't comprehend ... indeed he was stunned by what suddenly confronted him – rows and rows of grotesque looking foxes, each one eyeing him from the centre of a warped silvery screen.

Skulking Dog, of course, hadn't the faintest notion what these strange objects were. In fact, they were rows of gigantic aluminium mirrors, originally intended to reflect the sun and concentrate its rays so that its energy could be collected and stored. But the great mirrors had warped and, abandoned by the researchers, they now stood idle, reflecting only distorted images of the lawns and everything in them.

Frightened, Skulking Dog drew back. Running Fox grinned. 'Don't worry,' he said, 'These foxes won't harm you.'

'Who are they?' whispered Skulking Dog.

'Follow me,' said Running Fox, who was obviously enjoying himself very much. 'And don't get excited, whatever you do.'

Slowly they advanced towards the large mirrors, and as they did so, Skulking Dog saw the other foxes also advance and become huge and menacing.

Skulking Dog, needless to say, had often seen his own reflection in water. But he always felt on top of that situation, and anyway, it would disappear whenever he bit the water. However, when he bared his fangs and snapped at these foxes, they snapped back with even bigger fangs.

'Take it easy,' hissed Running Fox. 'It's only ourselves.'

Skulking Dog moved his head to one side, and so did some of the foxes in the mirrors opposite.

'Now, look at the others,' said Running Fox. 'That's me.'

'But you're all sorts of shapes.'

'And so are you,' laughed Running Fox. 'That's what those things do to you.'

'Come on,' said Skulking Dog. 'We're wasting our time. Let's see what we can do to help this other fox.'

As they crossed the fields on the way back to the trapper's house, Skulking Dog stopped.

'Wait a minute,' he said. 'Maybe we haven't been wasting our time. I've got an idea.'

The idea appealed to Running Fox and while he went on to the trapper's house to wait in the hope that he might be able to get a message to the fox in the shed, Skulking Dog returned to the badger set and told the others of his plan.

'If it doesn't work,' said Hop-along, who was always worried about anything that depended on having to run, 'then you'll all be killed.'

'At least,' said Black Tip, 'you'll have Running Fox to show the way.'

'And don't forget,' said Fang, 'Skulking Dog has experience of this sort of thing.'

'Still, you must take great care,' warned Vickey.

'Vickey's right,' said She-la. 'It would be a pity to come all this way just to end up as food for the howling dogs.'

There were clearly great dangers in the plan. At the same time Old Sage Brush didn't want to disappoint Skulking Dog. It was a good idea, and Skulking Dog undoubtedly had the courage to carry it through.

As he pondered on what to do, the old fox thought of the days when he had been able to lie and watch small flies creeping into the flowers of wild arum, there to be trapped until they could carry away the pollen. And so he expressed his approval in one of his quaint sayings.

'If a flower can catch a fly,' he told Skulking Dog, 'who is to say what the fox, with his cunning and speed, cannot do to the howling dogs?'

It was some time next morning when Running Fox came to tell Skulking Dog that the riders were gathering for the fox hunt, and he felt they should be on their way if they were to get into position in time. He had succeeded in getting a message to the fox in the shed when the trapper had gone out with his dogs to check his choking hedge-traps.

The night's frost had given way to a day of blue sky and fluffy white clouds, and the two foxes could feel the growing warmth of the sun on their backs as they raced across the fields. It wasn't long before the howling of the hounds and the call of the hunting horn could be heard coming across the country-side. It told them that the trapper had released his prisoner and that the hounds had picked up its scent. Immediately they split up so that they could put their plan into action.

As the pink-coated riders swept across the fields after the hounds, it might have occurred to them that the fox they were chasing was doing a strange thing. It was running straight into the wind and leaving a strong scent for the hounds to follow. In fact, although they may not have known it, the hounds were now following two foxes. Running Fox had joined the one that had been released and was showing it the way to the old mansion.

Meanwhile, Skulking Dog had taken up a position near the mansion. The bloodcurdling cry of the hounds and the incessant call of the horn were coming closer and closer. If Old Sage Brush had prayed for the success of his plan for the little brown hen, it was nothing to the fervent hopes of Skulking Dog now. What if his idea wouldn't work? Their very lives depended on it! Even as these fears were flooding into his mind, Running Fox streaked across the lawns, closely followed by a vixen. Skulking Dog joined them and together they darted under a low boxwood hedge and headed for the end of the mansion.

Hot on their heels, the hounds jumped over the boxwood hedge. But as they did so, they came face to face with the biggest and most fearsome creatures they had ever seen. They were tall, thin, fat, short, long and distorted in many other gruesome ways. Of course, the hounds had never got such a full and frightening view of themselves before, and for them this was the end of the hunt. With woeful howls, they turned tail and fled, bounding away between the horses and riders who had stopped in amazement in the low field beyond the edge of the lawns. Then, another strange thing happened.

In their flight across the lawns, the three foxes had accidentally bumped against the bottom of one of the reflectors, and now as it rocked to and fro, it flashed the sunlight onto the horses in the field below. First it dazzled one horse, then another, as they churned around in confusion. Startled, several of them reared up and threw their riders to the ground before galloping off across the fields at great speed.

In a wood on the other side of the mansion, Skulking Dog met the vixen he and Running Fox had just rescued. She was a pretty fox with an attractive little white spot on the centre of her forehead.

'Thank you,' she said. 'My name's Sinnéad.'

At gloomglow that evening, Running Fox led his visitors to the edge of his territory, and handed them over to the guidance of the great running fox in the sky. They wanted him to join them, but he seemed happy enough to stay where he was. And so, taking Sinnéad with them, they returned to Beech Paw.

EIGHT

Man's Work

In the brambles at the bottom of the quarry, a chaffinch gave a familiar whee and launched into a short song. In the den opposite, the foxes were happy too. All were delighted with the rescue of Sinnéad, and none more so than Old Sage Brush.

It was an emotional reunion between the old fox and his daughter. He had given her up for dead back at the sand pit, and now he was overcome. In his mind's eye he could still see her, a young cub snapping at the jabbing stick in an angry effort to protect her father's face. He would never see her as the mature vixen she now was, but it comforted him to think that at least he had seen her when she was young. As they rubbed cheeks affectionately, he could tell that she had grown into a fine fox, and although he couldn't see it, he could just imagine the attractive little white spot in the middle of her forehead.

Sinnéad was equally overjoyed. She also thought her father had died at the hands of the men with the jabbing sticks and the

107

snapping fun dogs. Her joy was tinged with sadness to see him old and blind. However, this soon gave way to a feeling of pride when she learned he was leading the others, and heard them speak of how much they owed to his great wisdom and cunning.

'But how did you survive?' Vickey asked her.

'Yes, how did you escape the men at the sand pit?' asked Skulking Dog. The others could see that he was greatly taken by the new vixen, and was showing more than a little interest in her.

Sinnéad looked at Skulking Dog with wide, soft eyes that showed she regarded him as nothing short of heroic for the way he had planned and carried out her rescue. 'Unfortunately,' she told him, 'I had no one like you to come to my aid. I was only a cub then.'

'That's all,' sighed Old Sage Brush. 'Just a cub.'

'Mother had just been shot,' continued Sinnéad. 'So she couldn't help me, and father couldn't see where he was running. I tried to follow him, but one of the men dived after me and caught me by the tail. I wriggled and squirmed. It was no use. I couldn't get free.'

'What did they do then?' asked Hop-along, who always wondered what would happen to him if he was caught.

'He held me up by the tail, and all the

other men gathered round, and the fun dogs jumped at me and snapped at my head. Somehow I managed to pull my head up and curl around to keep them from biting me, and the men laughed and thought it was great fun. Eventually they put me in a sack, like the ones we see in the potato fields, and carried me off. The fun dogs were still barking and snapping and nipping me.'

'Poor Sinnéad,' said Old Sage Brush. 'It must have been very frightening.'

Sinnéad nodded. 'The worst thing about it was that I couldn't see what was happening. The bag was rough and stuffy, and the smell of man so close to me was almost too much for me.'

'What happened then?' asked Vickey gently.

'After being bumped around in the sack for a long time, I was let out into a sort of cage. I think it must have been one of those places man keeps rabbits in. I tried everything to get out of it, but I just couldn't, and after a while I gave up. At least the smell of rabbit was better than the smell of man. Sometimes fun dogs would come along and scratch at the wire with their paws and bark at me. It was very frightening until I realised that if I couldn't get out, they couldn't get in.'

'What did you do for food?' asked Skulking Dog.

'Now and then the door was opened a little bit, and food was thrown in to me. Most of it was man's food, and I didn't like it. A few times I got chicken bones and bits of meat. It was barely enough to keep me alive, and I got very thin. Then one day the man came. I thought at first it was to give me food. However, he reached in to catch me. I snapped as much as I could, but he had something covering his hands and I didn't seem to hurt him. He caught me and put a thing around my neck and led me like a fun dog.'

'Oh, how horrible!' said She-la. 'Where did he take you?'

'He tried to get me to walk like a fun dog, and when I did something that pleased him he would give me a little piece of meat. He became quite good to me really. If a fun dog came along, he would take me up in his arms. Sometimes he would take me into places where there were a lot of men drinking and laughing and talking out loud. He would put me standing in one of the wooden things they sit on, and get me to snap at them, and he would get me to lick the stuff they were drinking. It was awful, and I always fought to get away from it. They seemed to think it was great fun.'

'Eventually, continued Sinnéad, 'the man grew tired of taking me around with him, and I was left in the cage. After that a woman fed me, and some children came to play with me. One day the children took me out and tried to put the thing around my neck, but they weren't as strong as the man and I was too quick for them. So I got away.'

'Good for you,' said Old Sage Brush. 'But how did man come to catch you again?'

'Well, after that I returned to the fields and kept as far away from man as I could. I managed to stay free until recently, when I was crossing the laneway leading to a farm. I got caught in a choking hedge-trap.'

'You poor thing,' said Vickey.

'I just don't know what happened,' said Sinnéad. 'I must have been thinking of something else. I walked straight into it.'

'How did you get out of it?' asked Black Tip in surprise.

'I was lucky again,' Sinnéad told them. 'For some reason it didn't choke me. I was caught in it, but it didn't tighten any more. Yet I couldn't get out of it. No matter how much I twisted and turned, I couldn't break it. I was terrified. I thought I was going to have to lie there and die of hunger. Then a man came along and a great fear came over me. I felt I was going to be killed. In desperation I pretended to be dead. I could feel his eyes on me. I didn't move. I didn't even breathe, and I couldn't believe my luck when he went away. I knew I must get out of that choking trap somehow before anyone else came along. I was really desperate, and I suppose that's how a woman came upon me unexpectedly. I was so busy trying to get that thing off my neck. I looked up and she was standing there looking down at me. I knew she would bring others, and I said this is the end now, I'm going to die. But the great god Vulpes was with me again. When the men came they didn't harm me. They caught me by the tail, cut the choking hedge-trap off my neck and put me in a sack.'

'So you ended up right back where you started,' said Fang. 'What happened after that?'

'I was kept in the sack and put into something hard and noisy, and moved a great distance. It was very bumpy and after a while I was taken out and given to another man who put me in a shed. You know the rest. I was held there until Running Fox came and told me of Skulking Dog's plan to get me away from the howling dogs. It was only then I realised what they were keeping me in the shed for.'

Sinnéad shivered, and added: 'I'd never have got away from them on my own – not in strange country.'

'Of course you would,' said Skulking Dog. 'You escaped before, didn't you?'

Sinnéad smiled. She knew he was just being generous. How lucky, she thought, not only to have got away, but to have met such a fine, strong fox as Skulking Dog. As a fox that had suffered much at the hands of man, Sinnéad was intrigued to learn that the others hoped to find the secret of survival.

'It's difficult to believe that such a thing is possible,' she said, wide-eyed with wonder.

'Some of the foxes who came to Beech Paw refused to believe it,' said Vickey. 'But Sage Brush is a very wise old fox now, and we believe what he says. We're tired of being hunted and killed.'

'Have you ever wondered why man hates us so much?' asked She-la. 'Surely his chickens can't mean that much to him.'

'We just don't know,' said Vickey. 'But do you realise that apart from yourself, Sinnéad, Running Fox was the first of our kind we met after we left Beech Paw?'

'I know,' said Sinnéad. 'There seems to be very few of us left. I had no mate at all last season, and no cubs.'

'That's why we've asked Old Sage Brush to help us,' said She-la. 'We feel that if we don't find the secret of survival, there'll be no more foxes left. Oh I do hope we find it, and that we aren't just chasing our tails.'

'We'll find it,' said Vickey firmly. 'We must find it. And when we do, we'll make Beech Paw a place where we can live without having to run all the time, where the hedgerows and the meadows hold no fear for us, where we can lie in the grass and watch our cubs

113

grow, knowing they'll live to enjoy freedom in the fields.'

'That would be nice,' reflected Sinnéad. She looked at Skulking Dog who was discussing the weather with the other dog foxes, and Vickey and She-la could see without being told, that she had decided to take him as her mate.

'Yes,' she smiled, 'that would be nice.' Pausing for a moment, she got up and announced: 'That settles it then. My cubs must also know how to survive.'

Having found her father and a mate she could be proud of, Sinnéad had more reason than any of them to want to learn the secret of survival. And now she had a dream. This little vixen, who had twice escaped from man, dreamt of the day when man would not be able to capture her again.

Somehow, spring and the new growth it would bring, seemed so long in coming, but it was coming. A small flower that had now made its appearance in the quarry told them so. The bright yellow star of the lesser celandine, rising above its heart-shaped, dark green leaves, seemed an appropriate messenger of spring to these creatures who followed the stars.

Unknown to Old Sage Brush and his group, the time of the choking hedge-traps was past for the moment. There was no demand for their coats, now that the breeding season had taken the lustre from their fur, and the trappers had put away their snares. Thus, as they set out from Beech Paw once more, they found it a welcome change to be able to follow the fox paths through the hedgerows without fear of being choked to death.

However, for the first time Vickey was worried. 'It's Old Sage Brush and Hop-along, she told the others. 'I think all this travelling is too much for them. She-la, you're Hop-along's mate. What do you think?'

'Well, to tell you the truth, Hop-along's not used to so much travelling. He hasn't said anything to me about it, but I think his fore-leg is beginning to pain him.'

'Old Sage Brush is slowing down too,' said Vickey.

'He's fairly frail,' Sinnéad reminded them, 'and his legs aren't as strong as they used to be.'

Black Tip nodded. He knew in his heart they were right.

'We're lucky no fun dogs have picked up our trail,' said Fang. 'If they did, I don't know what we'd do. We wouldn't be able to out-run them.'

'And we leave a strong scent,' said Skulking Dog. 'I know, I've been bringing up the rear.'

'What do you think we should do Vickey?' asked Black Tip. 'Return to Beech Paw?'

'If we could just rest up for a little while. The only thing is Old Sage Brush won't admit that he needs a rest.'

'The same with Hop-along,' said She-la.

'Then we must be cunning,' said Black Tip. 'Hasn't Old Sage Brush taught us that we should be?'

'What do you have in mind?' asked Fang.

'Vickey,' said Black Tip, 'you must tell Old Sage Brush that Hop-along's foreleg is paining him, and he needs a rest. And She-la, you must tell Hop-along that Old Sage Brush is tired, and that he needs a rest.'

The others smiled. Old Sage Brush couldn't have come up with a better idea himself. That way, both Old Sage Brush and Hop-along would be able to regain their strength and retain their pride by feeling they were helping one another.

Shortly after that their travels brought them to a small wooded valley. Its steep sides were cloaked in a tangle of bushes and undergrowth, a river flowed along the bottom of it, and between the river and one slope was a pheasant farm. What better place, they thought, to let Old Sage Brush and Hop-along rest. The cover was good, there was food in the undergrowth, and a prospect of pheasant if they were lucky.

As they made their way into the undergrowth, however, they got the distinct feeling that all was not well in the valley. There were no badgers, no rabbits and no foxes. In fact, all the holes they came to were blocked with stones.

'This place smells of death,' said Old Sage Brush. 'Tell me what you see, Black Tip?

'There are no fresh droppings, no scent.'

'So I've noticed. What else?'

'Stones block the entrances, and weeds grow on the pathways.'

'Man,' said the old fox.

'But the weeds tell us the danger has gone now,' said Vickey. 'Should we open up an earth and use it?'

'I don't like it,' said the old fox. 'What else do you see, Black Tip?'

'That's all. But you're right, it is man's work. He's left some of his rubbish behind.'

'Take me to it,' said Old Sage Brush.

Black Tip led him over to several empty cans lying around the entrance to a blocked-up earth. The old fox nudged them with his nose and sniffed them.

'What is it?' asked Vickey.

'I think it is something man uses to choke animals he doesn't like.'

'You mean, like choking hedge-traps?' asked Sinnéad.

'No, it comes from these things,' said Old Sage Brush, nosing one of the cans. 'When animals breathe it in, it chokes them. That's why man blocks up the holes – to keep them from getting out into the fresh air.'

The others stepped back quickly.

'It's all right, the old fox assured them. 'The danger has long since passed, but I'm afraid we cannot open up the earths again. The foxes who dug these earths still lie inside.'

'What will we do then?' asked Vickey.

'If man thinks foxes no longer live in this valley, then maybe it's the safest place we've found yet.'

'Sage Brush is right,' said Fang. 'The cover is good, so we've no need for an earth.'

'And there are pheasants down by the river,' Skulking Dog reminded them.

'No pheasants until we find out what the situation is,' warned Old Sage Brush. 'And certainly not before we're strong enough to run if we have to.'

Leaving the blocked-up earth, and the tell-tale cyanide cans that had been used to gas the occupants, they found a dry bed of withered grass beneath a protective umbrella of prickly brambles. By this time Old Sage Brush and Hop-along, with the encouragement of the others, were happy to rest, each pretending to believe it was for the benefit of the other.

Vickey and Black Tip lay on either side of the old fox to give him warmth, and soon he dozed off. As they watched his frail old body heave in deep sleep, they wondered how he had managed to keep going and how he would be able to continue. She-la was wondering the same about Hop-along as she licked his swollen fore-leg in an effort to soothe the pain. In spite of the many miles they had travelled, the others were in good shape, and after a while, when gloomglow had cast a comforting half-light across the valley, Black Tip got up to organise some food. Hop-along was asleep now too. All the better, he thought. No need to disturb him, or Old Sage Brush.

'Fang,' he whispered, 'you stay here. Keep an eye on Old Sage Brush and Hop-along. Skulking Dog, Sinnéad and She-la, you scout around and see if you can find any food. Don't go far, and remember what Old Sage Brush said, keep away from the pheasants. We're in no position to cope with any trouble. Vickey and I will circle the valley and see if we can find out what's been happening here.'

Quietly they stole away through the undergrowth in different directions. Skulking Dog and the two vixens found there was plenty of small food, including snails, frogs and rats, and having eaten their fill, they took some back to the others. Black Tip and Vickey also ate what food they could find, and went on to explore the valley. They crossed the river far above the pheasant

119

farm, where the water was shallow, circled through the bushes on the far side, and came back to the river again. There was no sign of any other foxes, or even badgers, and feeling somewhat disappointed, they edged their way down through a slippery gap in the bank to recross the river. As they did so, they suddenly found themselves looking into the small bright eyes of an otter. Startled, they stopped and stared.

Getting over his surprise, the otter twitched his short whiskered face and whistled softly. 'Forgive me,' he said, 'but I didn't expect to see any foxes here.'

'We've just arrived,' Black Tip told him.

'Where are you staying?' asked the otter.

'Across on the far side of the valley,' said Vickey. 'The others are waiting for us there.'

'You mean there are more?'

When they nodded, the otter whistled softly again, and warned: 'You must be careful. This valley holds great danger for foxes.'

'You mean the pheasant farm?' asked Black Tip.

'There are men there,' said the otter. 'And animals that will chase you,'

'Fun dogs,' said Vickey.

'But why do they hate us so?' asked Black Tip.

'We can't talk here,' said the otter. 'I too am in danger. Return to your friends, and I will come to you when it is safe.'

The otter slid down the mud into the river and swam ahead of them to the far bank. Having seen them safely across, he turned around and disappeared beneath the water.

Old Sage Brush and Hop-along were awake and enjoying food the others had brought them, when Black Tip and Vickey returned. A short time later, there was a soft whistle from the undergrowth, and a short whiskered face peeped in at them.

'It's Whiskers,' exclaimed Vickey, putting a name on yet another of her fellow-creatures.

There wasn't much room under the brambles, so they all came out into the clearing to hear what the otter had to say.

'Black Tip tells us you know what happened to the foxes who were here before us,' said Old Sage Brush.

Whiskers sat up on his hind legs, with his tail straight out behind him for balance. He twitched his whiskered snout and told them: 'Yes, it was the mink.'

'Mink?' asked the others.

'That's right,' said Whiskers. 'It escaped from a mink farm not far from here.'

'But how did that affect the foxes?' asked Black Tip.

Whiskers twitched his nose again. 'Greed. Just greed.'

Old Sage Brush eased himself down. 'Tell us about it, otter. What happened?'

Whiskers dropped to the ground and his

short forelegs brought his head low, giving him the manner of one who was about to confide in them.

'I used to have this valley to myself,' he told them. 'Well, myself and the foxes. Then the mink came. Before that we used to make an occasional raid on the pheasant farm. But we didn't over-do it. Just when we felt like a change of food, and the men and their – what did you call them? – fun dogs they didn't bother us too much. But when the mink came, it was different. The mink was too greedy. It raided the farm every night, stealing eggs and young pheasants. It got so bad that I couldn't go back there, and the foxes had to stay away too. If that wasn't bad enough, the men and their fun dogs came after us. They thought we were raiding the farm. I escaped up-river, but the foxes weren't so lucky – or the badgers, or anything else that lived around here. The men came and blocked up the holes and killed them.'

There was silence in the clearing, as the foxes felt the injustice of what had happened.

'Of course the mink escaped,' said Whiskers. 'But that's what I've come to warn you about. It's back!'

NINE

The Otter and the Mink

Daylight broke to reveal a valley that to all outward appearances was calm and peaceful. Rooks and wood-pigeons flew around the trees on the slopes above the pheasant farm, and down at the farm itself a hooded crow sat on the wire fence waiting his chance to go in and snatch some food. The chaffinches and sparrows felt no need to wait, and flitted in and out of the pens whenever they liked. Occasionally the harsh shriek of a cock pheasant shattered the stillness.

In the alder trees along the river, the small birds rested between their raids among drooping catkins and empty cones. Under the willows, which were now sprouting soft silvery buds, a tiny blue-tit hung upside down, showing his yellow underparts to the sky He was unconcerned with what was happening in the pheasant farm, and unaware of the drama that was soon to take place there.

In the woods above, the foxes pondered on what Whiskers the otter had told them. The fact that the mink was back in the valley was serious news. It meant that he would soon be raiding the pheasant farm again, and once he started that, the men and the fun dogs would be scouring the undergrowth looking for foxes. If that happened, they would be in trouble.

'Maybe we should move on,' said Fang, knowing that the inability of Old Sage Brush and Hop-along to run fast endangered them all.

Vickey, however, felt that the two weren't ready to move yet, and she wondered if the danger was so imminent as to require their departure immediately. 'Can't we wait just a little longer?' she asked.

'It would be a pity to move on without even one supper of pheasant,' said Skulking Dog.

'Even so,' said Black Tip. 'I agree with Fang. The moment the mink strikes again, we're in great danger.'

She-la thought it would be better for her mate, Hop-along to move on, however slowly, rather than risk a hopeless flight from the fun dogs. 'I think,' she said, 'we should go and make the most of it while we can.'

'Sinnéad?' asked Old Sage Brush.

Sinnéad tried to put a brave face on it. 'We've outrun fun dogs before.'

'Hop-along?'

'Maybe the others can – not me.'

'Nor me,' said Old Sage Brush.

'What do you want to do then?' asked

Black Tip.

The old fox thought for a moment. 'It's not what we want to do. It's what we have to do. As long as the mink is allowed to do as it pleases, no fox is safe in this valley.'

'Let me go after it,' urged Fang.

'And me,' said Skulking Dog. 'We'll soon drive it out.'

'That is not the way of survival,' Old Sage Brush told them. 'I admire your courage, Fang. And yours too, Skulking Dog. But what use will it be to us if one of you gets injured? The mink is small, but he is a savage fighter. We need all the strength and courage we have for the journey ahead.'

'What would you have us do then?' asked Vickey.

'Our brothers lie dead in the earth,' said Old Sage Brush. 'And we cannot hunt as we wish. Why? Because of the greed of a mink.' He rested his head between his forepaws. 'You ask me what we should do. Hasn't Vulpes shown us that the greedy fox who snaps off many heads when one will do, will lose his own? So also must the mink be shown that he – and he alone – must pay for his own greed.'

They all agreed that the mink should be made to pay. The question was how?

'If the mink is greedy,' said Old Sage Brush, 'he is not cunning. And if he is not cunning, then we must show him that we are.' He curled up and they could see he was still tired. 'I must sleep now. Black Tip, I'd like you to go and see the otter again at gloomglow. Talk to him. Find out all you can about the mink.'

Whatever their good intentions, the younger foxes should have known by this time that to run, even if they were able to do so, wasn't the old fox's way of doing things. Their concern was for each other, especially the weaker members of the group. His was a greater concern, a concern not only for themselves, but for any fox that might come to the valley when they had gone.

That night, as the others set out – Black Tip in search of the otter, the rest of them in search of food – Hop-along confided to Old Sage Brush that for the first time since they had left Beech Paw, he felt he might not be able to continue. His fore-leg was still swollen and sore, and he realised he was slowing them down.

'Maybe it would be best if She-la and I found a safe earth somewhere and stayed behind to rear our cubs,' he said.

Old Sage Brush could sense that Hop-along was feeling sorry for himself. Searching for the secret of survival was a difficult undertaking for a fox so handicapped as he was.

'Is this the Hop-along who joined us at Beech Paw?' asked the old fox. 'The Hop-along who out-jumped Lepus the Great and set us free in the Land of the Hares? The Hop-along that She-la has chosen above all other foxes? Surely my ears deceive me.'

'That first night at Beech Paw was a long time ago,' sighed Hop-along. 'I was stronger then.'

'So was I,' said Old Sage Brush. 'But if we have lost in strength, have we not gained in cunning? Has the great god Vulpes not shown us how to fox the little brown hen and turn back the howling dogs? Has he not shown us that even the very eye of gloom-glow is within our grasp, if we have the courage to reach out and take it? Surely we have not learned all of these things merely for a safe earth, but for all foxes, so that we can survive. How long would you and She-la survive here in a strange country and what about your cubs? No, Hop-along my friend, better that you stay with us. Soon you will be stronger again, and we are in need of you – and your cubs.'

Hop-along was quiet. Old Sage Brush had poured strength back into his heart, but his leg was still weak. Soon the other dogs and the vixens returned with food, and they wondered how Black Tip was doing down by the river.

In fact, Black Tip had found the otter without too much difficulty. Or was it the otter who had found him? He wasn't too sure. At

127

any rate, they met on the river bank. Whiskers was delighted to hear that the foxes were planning to do something with the mink, and he confided that he was working on a plan of his own. Maybe, he suggested, they could work together, as it was in both their interests to get the mink out of the way.

'Tell me about the mink,' said Black Tip. 'And your plan.'

'Well,' said the otter, 'there's not much to tell really.'

Black Tip was sitting on the bank watching the soft light of gloomglow flickering on the fast-flowing water. Whiskers went on: 'It came here round about your breeding time. The pheasants were starting to lay their eggs. I think it must have watched me. At first it couldn't get in to the pheasant farm. Then it got in the way I did.'

'How was that?' asked Black Tip.

'There's a small pond at one end.'

'Yes, I've seen it.'

'Well, a small stream flows into it, but the wire doesn't go right down to the bottom. I used to swim under it and get in that way.'

Black Tip smiled. It was so simple.

'The men at the farm never knew how I got in or out,' continued Whiskers. 'And as I told you before, I didn't go in too often – just now and then when I felt like a change. The river is my hunting ground and there's plenty of food for me there. But sometimes

128

I feel like having something different to eat.'

'I know how you feel,' said Black Tip. 'But go on.'

'One night when I arrived at the farm, I found that the mink had got in the same way. The pheasants were going mad, and I didn't dare go in. That was the start of it. The mink went in night after night, until the men got so annoyed they went up to the side of the valley and killed the foxes, badgers and everything they could find. I wouldn't mind, but the mink didn't need half the food it brought out.'

'How do you know?'

'Because I often found it, buried here, there and everywhere. It took so much it couldn't remember where it had hidden it.'

'Greed,' said Black Tip.

'That's right,' said Whiskers. 'Greed. The mink took more than it needed, and spoiled everything for everyone else.'

'Has it struck again yet?'

'Not yet. I saw it up-river not long ago. It's working its way down. It won't be long before it's here, and then you can look out. We can all look out. Nobody will be safe.'

'How will it get in?'

'The same way as before – under the wire. The men never discovered how it was getting in or out. They never even discovered it was the mink. They thought it was us.'

'When do you think it'll be here?'

The otter twitched his whiskered snout. 'When gloomglow comes again. Maybe a little longer.'

'Then we must move fast. What's your plan?'

'Follow me, and I'll show you.'

Dawn was breaking as Black Tip and Whiskers found a safe spot on the thickly wooded side of the valley from which they could look down on the pheasant farm. There were hundreds of buff-coloured hen pheasants, and a few brightly-coloured cocks. Black Tip couldn't help noticing how fat and well fed they looked, compared with the ones he hunted in the hedgerows.

The farm was a narrow strip of land sandwiched between the side of the valley and the river. It was fenced in and partly covered over with chicken wire, and the bottom of the fence was edged all around with sheets of shiny tin to keep foxes and other predators from gnawing their way in. At one end were the game-keeper's house and a shed where he took the eggs for hatching. The other end narrowed to the small pond where Whiskers – and later the mink – had got in. The pond was probably meant for ducks, thought Black Tip, although there were none there now. A shallow stream trickled down through a deep gully in the side of the valley into the pond, and a small dam held the water back from the river. Most of the pheasants were in the covered pens just inside the fence. A few more were in open pens in the centre, and Black Tip wondered why these didn't fly away.

'Sometimes they do,' Whiskers told him. 'But they always come back in for the food.'

'And what are those things for?' Black Tip was referring to four wooden poles that rose high above the pens at intervals outside the fence.

Whiskers explained that when raids started on the young pheasants, things on these poles lit up the whole area. 'It becomes so bright, he said, 'it's not safe to hunt.'

'Are there any shooters in the farm?'

'Not that I've seen.'

'How many fun dogs are there?'

'One for each leg of your body.'

Black Tip didn't like the sound of that. 'Don't they touch the pheasants?'

Whiskers shook his head. 'They don't seem to be interested in them. I often see them running around when the men are putting out food and water for the pheasants, and they don't chase them or bother with them.'

'What a strange way for fun dogs to act,' mused Black Tip.

'Don't let that fool you,' warned Whiskers. 'They hunt everything else – rabbits, foxes, even me when they get the chance.'

As Black Tip looked down on the pheasant

farm, he just couldn't imagine how they were going to teach the mink a lesson. Maybe, he thought, Fang and Skulking Dog were right, and the only answer was to attack the mink and frighten it away. Yet, when they suggested simply going in and attacking something, Old Sage Brush always said there was another way. Indeed, with the old fox and Hop-along back up there in the undergrowth, they would have to think of another way. They couldn't risk a noisy fight that would frighten the pheasants and bring out the fun dogs. The dogs would soon pick up their scent, and there would be no question of survival, at least, not for some of them. No, there had to be some other way.

'You said you had a plan,' said Black Tip.

Whiskers nodded. 'The fun dogs can't find out where the mink is getting in and out because it goes under the water.'

'So?'

'So I'm going to let the water out.'

'How?' asked Black Tip.

'I'm digging a hole through the dam from the river. I've been at it some time and I'm nearly finished. The thing is, I need your help.'

'How can I help you?'

Whiskers thought for a moment. 'If I let the water out of the pond after the mink goes into the farm, and if you then raise the alarm while it's still in there, the fun dogs

132

could follow it out, as there'd be no water to stop them.'

The plan appealed to Black Tip's natural cunning. At the same time, his sense of self-preservation made him realise the dangers involved. 'The problem is,' he said, 'how can we raise the alarm without drawing the fun dogs on to our own trail?'

Clearly Whiskers was relying on the foxes to provide the answer to that. Black Tip promised to contact him again when they had decided what they could do to help, and returned to the others. Knowing the danger the valley held for them, Vickey was anxiously awaiting him, and hopped out into the clearing to greet him. They rubbed noses affectionately for a moment, and then she took him into where Old Sage Brush and Hop-along were still talking.

'Well, what do you think we should do?' asked Old Sage Brush when Black Tip had told them.

'I'm not sure yet.'

'Hop-along,' said the old fox. 'You fooled Lepus the Hare. What do you think we should do?'

'If the fun dogs are not to follow us, then we must leave no trail,' said Hop-along. 'And the only way we can do that is by using the river.'

'That's what I was thinking,' said Black Tip. 'The answer must lie in the river.'

'Very well then,' said Old Sage Brush, 'Think about it. As your minds are in agreement, the answer will be easier to find.'

It was coming on towards evening when a soft whistle from the undergrowth announced the arrival of Whiskers. The mink was on its way to the pheasant farm, he told them. By this time the swelling on Hop-along's leg had gone down, and he felt much stronger. So much so that he was able to go out with Black Tip and Whiskers to the same spot overlooking the farm where they could watch the mink.

It wasn't long before they spotted the little animal. It had dark brown fur and, the foxes thought, was rather like an otter, only smaller. Running along the outside of the fence, it stopped now and then to rise up and look in over the sheets of tin that edged the wire. On reaching the stream, it dived in and a few moments later popped up in the pond on the inside. So quietly did it make its way up along the pen, that many of the pheasants didn't even notice it.

'What do you think?' asked Whiskers. 'Can you do it without being caught yourselves?'

'We were thinking that the only way to leave no trail is to use the river,' said Hop-along.

'Or perhaps the stream,' said Black Tip.

'That's it,' said Hop-along. 'We could walk along it and leave no trail for the fun dogs to follow.'

'Good,' smiled Whiskers. 'And I'm almost through the dam.'

Because of the mink's raid on the farm, there was now the real danger that the men might come looking for foxes again. So when Black Tip and Hop-along returned to the others, it was decided to put the plan into operation as soon as possible. The vixens wanted to take part, but it was also decided not to put them and their unborn cubs at risk. Consequently, it was agreed that Old Sage Brush and the vixens would wait at the bend on the river below the pheasant farm, and the younger dogs would take care of the mink.

Before dawn, Old Sage Brush and the vixens left. Black Tip went with them part of the way, then veered off to find out how Whiskers was getting on. From the vantage point overlooking the farm, he could see that the otter was busy working on the far side of the dam. Everything was going according to plan. Later, Hop-along, Fang and Skulking Dog joined him, and they settled down to wait for the mink's return, knowing that greed would bring it back again that night.

As the light began to fade, the four dog foxes made their way down along the stream until they were almost beside the pond, and concealed themselves under the bank. Whiskers darted up around from the river to tell them he was all set. They waited. A short time later they spotted the furtive movement of the brown furry mink making its way along the bottom of the fence towards them. Unaware that it was being watched, it dived under the wire and made its way up through the pen. At the same time the foxes could see a small whirlpool forming at the far end of the pond as the water began to swirl out. Whiskers had broken through.

'Now Hop-along, whispered Black Tip. 'Now.'

One by one they followed Hop-along up out of the stream. He and Black Tip went one way, Fang and Skulking Dog the other. Running around the fence, they stopped now and then to jump up against the wire and bark at the pheasants. Immediately the birds in the enclosed pens scattered in panic and finding no way of escape, flapped furiously against the wire, while those in the open pens rose into the air with loud screeches and flew down the river.

The mink stopped what it was doing and looked up to see what all the commotion was about. The men and their dogs ran from the house, knowing they had an intruder. Hidden from sight, first by the sheets of tin along the bottom of the fence, and then by the steep sides of the gully, the foxes quickly made their way back up into the undergrowth.

When the mink returned to the pond, it

was as if someone had pulled the plug from a bath. Only a trickle of water remained. It darted across the mud and out under the wire. This time, however, the dogs could not only see it getting out, they could follow it. They were close on its tail, and as the foxes left the stream and ran away through the bushes, they could hear from the excited barking down at the farm, that the mink was cornered. Pausing briefly to look back, they saw that it had scaled one of the high wooden poles, curled itself around the top, and was snarling viciously down at the dogs and the men who had now joined them.

Whiskers had already floated down the river and was with Old Sage Brush and the vixens when the others arrived. He sat up on his hind legs and gave a long low whistle of delight. The foxes smiled. From the direction of the pheasant farm, they could still hear the fun dogs barking, and in the gloom they could just make out the shape of the mink curled around the top of the pole. The plan had worked well. Very soon, they knew, the mink would be back in the mink farm. With it out of the way, Whiskers would have the river to himself, and some day perhaps, other foxes would come and live in the valley again. In the meantime, as Skulking Dog reminded them, there were pheasants to be found in the undergrowth.

TEN

Facing the Fun Dogs

A faint scattering of yellow blossoms now
sparkled on the gorse like stardust. New
daisies, small and streaked with pink, pushed
their heads up into the cold spring air. Here
and there, dark green circles of fresh grass
ringed the spot where last year the cattle had
manured the fields. In the hedgerows, the
sight of small buds brought a hopeful note
from the pink-breasted bullfinch.

The raid on the pheasant farm, and the
defeat of the mink, had gladdened the
hearts of the foxes considerably, especially
Hop-along. By including him in the plan
and getting him to lead the way, Old Sage
Brush and Black Tip had succeeded in
giving him the encouragement he needed to
continue. He was also well rested now, and
his foreleg was much stronger. The others
could see that Old Sage Brush was feeling
stronger too.

Their meeting with Whiskers, the otter,
had been a most enjoyable experience. As a
creature who was also hunted by man and
his dogs, they had found they had much in

common with him. They had also come to admire the skill with which he hunted, both in and out of the water, and before leaving him on the bend of the river, had thanked him in a way that showed they regarded him as an equal. For his part, Whiskers wished them well in their search for the secret of survival, before sliding silently into the water to return to his old haunts.

Leaving the pheasant farm behind, they had followed the brush further north, and as they rested up during the day they became aware of more signs of spring than they had seen for a long time. Of all these, the most meaningful to them was the sprinkling of yellow blossoms on the gorse. When the bushes were in full bloom, they knew the time would have come for the vixens to give birth to their cubs. That was still some while away, but the yellowing of the gorse was enough to make Black Tip uneasy about the vixens, especially Vickey.

'There are always some blossoms on the gorse,' said Old Sage Brush when they told him. 'Are you sure these are new?'

'I'm sure,' Black Tip replied.

'He's right, said Hop-along. 'It's only a matter of time now before Vickey and She-la become heavy with cubs, and when that happens we must settle them in a safe earth.'

Fang agreed. He was the only dog, apart

139

from Old Sage Brush, of course, not to have taken a mate. But he fully understood.

'Then we must do what my eyes tell me to do,' Old Sage Brush announced. 'We must return to Beech Paw.'

'And what about the secret of survival?' asked Skulking Dog.

'Who knows what secrets we have learned?' replied the old fox. 'Come, we must tell the vixens.'

Old Sage Brush was now anxious that they should be on their way as soon as possible. From what Black Tip had told him, the weather looked as if it might change. He wanted to cover as much ground as they could while the brush could still be seen, so as soon as the running fox climbed into the sky, they turned their backs to it and set off.

Black Tip, however, had read the signs well for his old leader. After a short time the clouds closed in, obscuring the moon and the stars, and it started to rain. They were all aware of the danger of travelling without either the light of gloomglow or the brush to guide them. However, the breeding instinct was now uppermost in their minds, and it told them that whatever the dangers, they must press on. Soon they found themselves in hill country. None of them could recall having come through these hills on the way from Beech Paw, but it was only because they couldn't see the brush that they wondered if they were on the right track.

Making their way up the side of a hill covered with bracken and patches of gorse, they came across a fox path, and in the hope that whatever fox had used it might be able to tell them where they were, they decided to follow it. There was no fresh scent on the path, but it was clearly still in use. Less clear was the choking hedge-trap it led to.

As usual Black Tip was in the lead just ahead of Old Sage Brush. Following the path through a hole in a hawthorn hedge, he suddenly found himself yanked off his feet. Realising he was the victim of a choking hedge-trap, he made a desperate effort to squirm free. The more he struggled, the tighter the wire closed around his neck, choking him. Vickey and Sinnéad were at his side in an instant.

'Don't move,' whispered Sinnéad in his ear. 'The more you struggle, the worse you'll make it.'

'Sinnéad's right,' said Vickey 'She knows what these things are like. Just lie still and we'll try and get you out.' Vickey was very upset by the plight of her mate. Indeed, they were all upset to see one so brave as Black Tip held tight in the grip of an enemy he could not fight.

'Let's not panic,' Old Sage Brush spoke firmly 'Black Tip, can you hear me?'

Black Tip could hear the voice of his old

master, but only vaguely, as if in a dream. The wire of the snare was cutting into his throat, choking him, and squeezing his eyes until he couldn't see.

'He can hear you all right, said Vickey, 'but he cannot answer. Tell me what you want, and I will be your eyes until we set him free.'

'Describe it to me,' said Old Sage Brush, 'so that I may see it in my mind's eye.'

The darkness was now giving way to a dull grey dawn, and they knew that they must act quickly. There was no scent of man in the vicinity of the trap. If that meant it was just one a trapper had set and then forgotten, they were all right, but it could also mean it was being left until the scent of man had disappeared, in which case it would be checked soon.

Unlike a rabbit snare, which is usually made of a thin copper wire tied to a short wooden stake driven into the ground, this was a much sturdier trap. It was made of a fairly heavy chain about a foot long, and two strong wires that were twisted around each other for added strength.

Where the wire joined the chain there was a swivel, so no matter how much a fox might twist and turn, the snare would not break, but merely turn with it. Furthermore, whoever had put it in the hedge, had secured it to the sturdy stump of a hawthorn bush, knowing well that a fox would be able to pull a wooden stake from the ground.

With the help of the others, especially Sinnéad, Vickey gave the old fox this picture of the choking hedge-trap that had snared her mate, and when they had finished he told them: 'If we can't get it off his neck, then we'll have to bite through whatever it's tied to.'

They could all see for themselves now this was the only way, so while Vickey tried to get her teeth under the wire around Black Tip's neck, the others took turns at gnawing the hawthorn stump. It was difficult. They had to work in the middle of the hedge and there wasn't much room. Black Tip's head wasn't far from the stump, and Vickey was in there too trying to loosen the snare. This meant that they could only chew at the stump one at a time.

Anxiously Old Sage Brush lay and listened. He could tell from the sound of their exertions that they were working feverishly. At the same time, he knew from what they were saying to each other that they weren't making much progress, either with the stump or the snare. Black Tip was also listening. Having calmed himself, he could feel the blood flowing more freely through his veins again, and there was less pressure on his eyes. Even so, the wire was still cutting deeply into his neck, and he knew Vickey just couldn't get her teeth under it.

Daylight came. Under the hedge, the flattened grass showed how hard the foxes had wrestled to free their friend. They had succeeded in tearing good-sized strips off the hawthorn stump, yet in spite of all their efforts it still stood, tough and unyielding, stubbornly refusing to give up its prisoner. Black Tip had sufficiently recovered now to lie and watch them. Tired as they were, he could see they had no thought of giving up. He knew, however, what they were not prepared to admit. They were wasting their time.

'Vickey,' he whispered at long last.

Vickey lowered her head so that she could hear him. 'Yes, Black Tip.'

'You must go now. Soon man will come, and his fun dogs. You must go.'

'We won't leave you,' Vickey told him. 'Don't worry, we'll soon have you free.'

'Tell Old Sage Brush I want to speak to him.'

Vickey brought the old fox over.

'Sage Brush,' croaked Black Tip. 'You must take Vickey and the others and go now.'

'I cannot travel without my eyes,' said Old Sage Brush.

'If you stay here we will all die,' replied Black Tip.

Old Sage Brush nodded. He knew Black Tip was right. From the time they had set out from Beech Paw, they had planned

144

everything in such a way that some of them at least would survive. That was still the most important thing.

'Take the vixens on to Beech Paw,' Black Tip urged him. 'Fang and Skulking Dog can help me. We'll catch up with you.'

Vickey thought desperately. She couldn't abandon Black Tip to man and his fun dogs. Yet what could she do? If only she could get her teeth under the wire that held him so tightly by the neck. She thought of the day when Fang lay wounded in the hollow beside the frozen steam and how water from Black Tip's mouth had released him from death's grip. Suddenly, as she thought of the water dripping on to the powerful fangs that had fought so bravely for her, she had an idea.

'Fang,' she said. 'Fang can do it.'

'Don't waste any more time,' said Black Tip.

Vickey appealed to Old Sage Brush. 'It's worth a try,' she pleaded. 'Fang has longer teeth than any of us.'

Hearing Vickey speak his name, Fang was by their side in an instant.

'Well, Fang,' asked Old Sage Brush. 'Can your teeth find the wire?'

Fang lay down beside the young dog who had fought him, then given him back his life; the young dog he had since come to admire so much. Could he do the same for him? Gently he started probing for the choking wire. It was buried deep in the fur and flesh of Black Tip's neck. The others stood around, waiting anxiously. Fang put his head to one side. He could just feel the wire. Curling his lip back to get as much length on his teeth as possible, he pressed down as far as he could. Black Tip twitched and braced himself against the pain.

'Go on Fang,' Vickey urged. 'You can do it.'

Fang eased his long front teeth a little lower, then lower still. Black Tip flinched again.

'Hold on,' whispered Vickey. 'I think he has it.'

Fang turned his head slightly, and he could feel one of his fangs sliding under the wire. Gently he tried to ease it back. It didn't move. He pulled on it again. This time it opened up a little, then a little more. Now Vickey was able to get her teeth under the wire, and together they opened the snare. Black Tip squirmed back out of it. He was free.

They all turned and ran up the hill to the cover of some gorse. The reappearance of the choking hedge-traps had taken them by surprise. It was the last thing they had expected, as the traps had disappeared after they had left Running Fox in the Land of the Howling Dogs. The question was, why had they come back to the hedgerows now?

It was a question that worried Old Sage Brush, and he asked Fang and Skulking Dog to scout around and see what they could find out. While they were away, Vickey could tend to Black Tip's wounded throat, and with luck he would be sufficiently recovered by gloomglow to continue.

Fang and Skulking Dog set off in a wide circle. They found they were in the country of the hill sheep, a country that was wild and rugged and suitable for nothing else. Hill sheep have their lambs later than those on low-lying farms and the presence of hooded crows in unusual numbers suggested it was either lambing time here, or there were sheep in trouble. In fact, it turned out to be both. They soon came across some pregnant ewes entangled in thorn hedges and barbed wire fences, and in one field hooded crows scattered from the carcasses of two dead sheep. The sheep had been torn open, and they knew immediately this was the work of marauding dogs.

Like the hooded crows, foxes are also carrion eaters, of course, and while Fang and Skulking Dog recognised the danger of delaying, it was not in their nature to forego such an opportunity to eat. They had worked long and hard during the night to free Black Tip, and they were hungry. There was plenty of meat on the dead sheep, and

147

they couldn't believe their good fortune in having found food so easily.

What Fang and Skulking Dog didn't realise was that they had also found the reason for the reappearance of the choking hedge-traps. A pack of marauding dogs had been causing much trouble in the area. Such dogs are a danger to sheep at any time of year, but when they kill pregnant ewes, the farmers are at the loss of the lambs too. The hill farmers also knew that foxes were likely to appear at lambing time. So, while the men who trapped for furs had taken in their snares, the farmers had put out theirs. Furthermore, some of them had now taken to carrying their shotguns in the hope that they would come across the dogs that were causing all the trouble.

The first Fang and Skulking Dog knew that a farmer had spotted them at the dead sheep, was when shotgun pellets whined over their heads. The hooded crows which had been waiting and watching like vultures on a nearby fence, wheeled away out of range. Fang and Skulking Dog sprang to life and raced for cover. Quickly the farmer reloaded and fired again as they streaked through the nearest hedge. Fortunately, he too had been taken by surprise, and his aim wasn't good. Both escaped without so much as one pellet in their pelt. Realising how lucky they had been, they circled widely again and returned to the others.

'I was afraid it might be something like that,' said Old Sage Brush when they told him about the dead sheep and the farmer. 'Are you sure you weren't followed here?'

They assured him they hadn't been, and the old fox announced that they must leave the area without delay. The farmer or his sheepdogs might come looking for them. Worse still, the fun dogs that were running wild and attacking the sheep might find them, and dogs like that, with a taste for killing, would be a great danger. Black Tip now felt well enough to travel, so they slipped silently out of the gorse.

Taking care to avoid any choking hedge-traps that might now lie in their path, they continued in what they hoped was the general direction of Beech Paw. Old Sage Brush had taken the precaution of getting Fang and Skulking Dog to bring up the rear, and when they had stopped to rest, he also asked Fang to circle behind them to make sure they weren't being followed. Fang found nothing, but the old fox wasn't happy, and a short time later he sent Skulking Dog out. When Skulking Dog returned, he sought out Fang and told him: 'Old Sage Brush must have sensed something. I think the fun dogs have picked up our trail.'

Fang sat up. 'You mean the farmer's dogs?'

'I don't think so. They're running in a

pack. I'd say they're the ones that have been attacking the sheep. What do you think we should do? I don't want to alarm the others.'

'We'll tell Old Sage Brush and Black Tip,' said Fang. 'They'll know what to do.'

On hearing the news, Old Sage Brush was thoughtful for a moment. 'I had a feeling we were being followed,' he said. 'How far back are they?'

'A good way,' Skulking Dog told him. 'We've left enough circles and false scents to keep them busy for a while.'

'Good,' said the old fox, 'but we better move on. Say nothing to the others for the moment. Skulking Dog, you and Fang stay here at the rear, and let me know if they get close.'

'I'll stay back too,' Black Tip volunteered. 'I'm okay now.'

'All right,' said Old Sage Brush. 'Vickey can be my eyes. We need all the strength we can muster back here in case the fun dogs catch up with us.'

'But how can we travel without the brush to guide us?' asked Skulking Dog.

'We'll just have to keep going and hope we don't go off course,' said Old Sage Brush. 'Hurry. We've no time to waste.'

If the others suspected something was wrong, they said nothing, and with Vickey leading, they continued their journey by daylight. Every now and then one of the foxes bringing up the rear, doubled back to check. In this way they were able to lay more false scents which they hoped might delay their pursuers or put them off their trail altogether. However, their efforts were in vain. There were too many of them travelling together, and they were leaving a strong scent. As the morning wore on, it became apparent that the fun dogs were gaining on them. They were now approaching an area where plantations of evergreens capped the hills, and lakes shimmered in the meadows below.

'Maybe we could make it to those evergreens,' suggested Skulking Dog.

'They're too far away,' said Black Tip, 'but there's a small wood just ahead of us. We could make a stand there and let the others try and reach the evergreens.' Skulking Dog nodded, and Fang said: 'All right, let's tell them to make a run for it. Hurry, there's no time to lose.'

By now the vixens had sensed that something was wrong, and the news that they were being followed came as no surprise to them. They took off as fast as they could for the wood, closely followed by Hop-along and Old Sage Brush.

For once Old Sage Brush felt helpless, and as the other three caught up with them at the edge of the wood and told them their plan, he asked sadly: 'Why must it end like this, my gallant young friends? Why?'

'Because this is the way it has to be,' said Black Tip.

'I stay because I have nothing to lose,' said Fang.

'And we stay because we have everything to lose if we don't,' said Skulking Dog. 'At least our vixens and our cubs will survive.'

They parted in a clearing in the middle of the wood. There was no time for sorrow. The fun dogs were closing in. A touch of noses, a look that said thanks, and the others were on their way. Then the three dog foxes lay down to wait for a fight they knew they could not win, either by courage or cunning.

There were four dogs in the pack – a young alsatian and three small mongrels. They were town dogs nobody cared about. The white one with the black ear had been a boy's pet until he tired of it. The long-bodied brown one had belonged to an old woman who had died. The scruffy black one had never belonged to anyone. In the alsatian they had found a leader and in the sheep flocks of the country all of them had found a lot of fun. However, chasing sheep was a game that had given them a taste for blood and turned harmless stray dogs of the streets into a savage pack of hunters with a price on their heads.

The three foxes lay among the bracken in the clearing. Behind them, the others had gone off through the trees to safety. Ahead of them they could hear the fun dogs panting as they plodded through the undergrowth in pursuit of their quarry. An excited bark from the alsatian, and a squeal of delight from one of the smaller dogs, told them the time had come. Their normal instinct was to run, but they knew that if they evaded capture the fun dogs might return to the scent of the others, and they couldn't risk that. It had to be a fight.

As the dogs raced into the clearing, the three foxes sprang out of the bracken and leaped on the alsatian. The three mongrels flung themselves into the battle, and the quietness of the clearing was shattered by a rolling, snapping, shrieking ball of fury. Skulking Dog was hanging out of the alsatian's neck when he felt a searing pain in his tail and was forced to release his grip and fight off the brown dog. Fang turned to snap at the white dog with the black ear as it sank its teeth into his right hind leg. Black Tip turned to face the scruffy black dog and would have died in the jaws of the alsatian were it not for the fact that he and the black dog rolled over and over so fast the alsatian couldn't catch him. The alsatian was standing waiting ... waiting for the opportunity to snap its powerful jaws on one of them. When that happened, it would be all over.

So intent was the alsatian in watching for its chance, that it failed to see the three vixens streaking out of the undergrowth and launching themselves at its neck. As they fell to the ground, snarling and snapping, the noise in the clearing reached a frightening pitch. The three smaller dogs who were locked in battle with the young dog foxes, saw the alsatian go down and immediately their courage began to flag. To add to the confusion, two more foxes had appeared. Hop-along was in there with the vixens, seeking a grip on the alsatian's throat too. The smaller dogs weren't to know that the vixens were in cub, that Hop-along was lame, and that the last fox to appear at the edge of the clearing was blind. All they knew was that their leader was down and they were suddenly out-numbered. Disentangling themselves from their attackers, they turned and fled. The alsatian now found itself alone and in serious danger of being overcome. Shaking off its attackers, it too beat a hasty retreat.

Hardly able to believe their good fortune, the foxes gathered themselves up. They were a sorry sight. Sage Brush, old and frail. Hop-along, hobbling on three legs. The vixens, one obviously in cub and all badly shaken. Black Tip, bruised and bleeding and with the mark of the snare around his neck. Skulking Dog, the tip of his tail almost bitten off. Fang, dragging his torn right hind leg. Nevertheless, they were alive, and in case the fun dogs might pick up the courage to resume the attack, they limped off through the trees as fast as they could.

ELEVEN

A Wrong Turn

In the depth of the evergreens, the dog foxes licked their wounds. The flight from the fun dogs had taken a lot out of Old Sage Brush, and he soon dozed off. Black Tip was unable to get his tongue round to soothe the bruise that circled his neck, so Vickey did it for him. The choking hedge-trap had bitten deep, deeper even than the teeth of the fun dogs, and his neck was stiff and sore. Drops of dried blood here and there on his hair showed where the wire had seared its way through his thick coat, and Vickey cleaned them off and smoothed the fur back into place.

Fang's right hind leg was also stiff and sore from the bite he had got. The little white dog had sunk its teeth well and truly into his hip as he was busy engaging the alsatian. It had drawn blood and caused him considerable pain, but as he licked his wounded leg he was determined to be on the move again soon because he knew delay would only make movement more difficult.

Skulking Dog's only injury was to his tail.

The brown dog had sunk its teeth right into the bone, and instead of the brush being full and flowing like it should be, the end of it was matted with blood and was bent in a most unfoxlike fashion. He cleaned the wound and tried to nudge the tip back into position. But each time he flicked it, it bent again. Sinnéad, who was watching, thought it was most peculiar, and went over to see if she could nudge it into position. Back, however, it would not go, and after several unsuccessful efforts she stepped back, cocked her head to one side and looked at it. It did look funny, she thought, and suddenly she felt like laughing. However, she knew if she did she would only hurt her mate's feelings, so she just smiled and said: 'Don't worry, Skulking Dog, it'll be as good as new in no time.'

Hop-along, who was poking his nose under a flat rosette of plantain leaves in search of slugs, lifted his head and sniggered. The others looked up and smiled. Somehow the sight of a fox with a bent brush made them forget their own troubles for a moment. It looked very strange. Skulking Dog grinned. He was glad to see them laughing again, even if it was at his expense.

The sniggering stirred Old Sage Brush out of his slumber, and as Fang came over and settled down beside him, he observed: 'You limp.'

The others looked at the old fox, surprised that he could tell the difference in Fang's trot on the soft grass. He might be blind, they thought, but the sharpness of his hearing was matched only by the sharpness of his mind.

'I'll be all right, said Fang. 'Just a bit sore after the fight with the fun dogs.'

'And how are the rest of you?' asked Old Sage Brush. 'Vickey, you shouldn't have gone back to fight the fun dogs. Nor you, She-la.'

In fact, Vickey was a bit worried since their fight with the fun dogs. She had been thrown to the ground rather heavily by the alsatian, and she was concerned in case her unborn cubs might have been hurt. Yet it was a fear she hadn't shared with anyone, not even Black Tip. Somehow she felt that at this stage it was a matter entirely for herself. Later, when the cubs were born, there would be a time for sharing. Until then she would keep her fears to herself and wait her time.

'I'm all right,' she told Old Sage Brush.

'So am I,' said She-la.

'And Sinnéad?' he asked. 'How about you?'

'I'm fine too,' she said.

'Don't worry,' Vickey assured him. 'We're all right.'

'That's good,' said the old fox. 'But you shouldn't have put your cubs at risk.'

'It's just as well they did,' said Black Tip, 'or we wouldn't be here now.'

'That's right,' said Skulking Dog. 'We'd never have fought off the fun dogs on our own.'

'You didn't have to come back either,' said Fang to Old Sage Brush. 'Or you Hop-along. But you did.'

The two dog foxes didn't reply, so Vickey said: 'Anyway we had no choice. If the fun dogs had killed you, they'd have come after us. So we only did what we had to do.'

'I'm glad you did,' said Black Tip, and nothing more was said about the matter as this seemed to sum up the feelings of all of them.

'And how about you Black Tip?' asked Old Sage Brush.

'No injuries,' said Black Tip. 'My neck's a bit sore still from the choking hedge-trap. That's all. Hop-along's all right too. So's Skulking Dog, except that he's got a bent brush.'

Old Sage Brush chuckled. In his mind's eye he could just imagine it, and he repeated: 'A bent brush?' and chuckled again to himself.

'My brush may be bent,' said Skulking Dog, 'but there's nothing wrong with my hearing.'

'Sorry,' said Old Sage Brush. 'I didn't mean to laugh. The important thing is that you're all right.'

The others didn't hear the old fox chuckle again, but they got the distinct impression he did. Old and all as he was, he could still enjoy the thought of a fox with a bent brush, and they were glad to see him smile. The rest was doing him good already.

Black Tip couldn't help thinking that while they could laugh at their fight with the fun dogs now, it had been no laughing matter at the time. He also wondered and not for the first time, if in fact Old Sage Brush had deliberately misled the fun dogs into thinking there were only three foxes so that the surprise of seeing the others, rather than their strength, would win the day. He thought of asking him, then changed his mind. He didn't think the old fox would tell him, and anyway, some things, he felt, were better left unsaid.

As they waited for darkness, they amused themselves by recalling their adventures since they had started searching for the secret of survival. Sinnéad was thrilled to hear how her father had manoeuvred the little brown hen so as to get food out of the hatchery in the hollow; and how Hop-along had outwitted Lepus in the Land of the Hares. Privately she was delighted that Skulking Dog's encounters with the howling dogs and the fun dogs had equalled those feats in cunning and courage. Some day in the not-too-distant future she would be telling her cubs about the daring way he had rescued her, and how he had fought for her. Skulking Dog would be a father they could be proud of.

Soon they fell asleep, and when they awoke they found themselves enveloped in the comfort of darkness. It was raining again, and the clouds still hid the brush from view. However, they were anxious to put as many fields as possible between themselves and the fun dogs, so they pressed on and didn't stop until they came to a river.

Hearing the patter of rain on the water, Old Sage Brush asked: 'Which way does the river run?'

'I can't make out which way it flows answered Black Tip. 'It hardly seems to move at all.'

They had never come across a river like this before. The banks were flat and straight, and on exploring it for a short distance they found there were many waterfalls and bridges along the way, but no bushes or ditches to slow them down. Instead, there were paths that would allow them to make good progress, and there were long stretches of reeds where they could hunt for moorhens and other food as they went along. Unable to see if the brush was still behind them they decided to follow the river in the hope that it might lead them towards Beech Paw

Unknown to the foxes, they had strayed far from Glensinna. In travelling without the brush to guide them, and in their efforts to escape from the fun dogs, they had turned full circle, and instead of going back towards Beech Paw, they were going farther away from it.

Thus, their flight from the fun dogs had taken them up through the hills to the south of Dublin, and the river they had come upon was in fact the Grand Canal which cuts across the country from the River Shannon to Dublin. As a result, they were now going towards a bigger concentration of man than they had ever known.

Unaware of this mistake, they continued the journey along the river without interruption, apart from stops to allow Old Sage Brush and Hop-along to rest. Once or twice they also paused to listen when they thought a fun dog might have picked up their trail, but each time it came to nothing. It was something else that gave Old Sage Brush a feeling that all was not well. The sound of falling water told them they had come to another wooden crossing. Old Sage Brush stopped and sniffed the air. 'What's that smell?' he asked.

'I think it must be man's rubbish,' said Black Tip.

Now, as they peered through the darkness,

they could see heaps of rusty cans and broken bottles in off the pathway, and pieces of wood and plastic containers floating at the edge of the water. There were two or three horses grazing along the banks, but they knew they were no longer in the country. Beyond the horses they could make out the shapes of buildings, and above the noise of the waterfall the barking of fun dogs now came to their ears.

'We've gone far enough,' said Old Sage Brush turning back. 'This is man's place.'

A smelly river bank so near man was the last place any of them expected to meet another fox. But man's place was also the hunting ground of a mangy little fox called Scavenger, and he had picked up their scent some way back. Seeing the country foxes turning and retracing their steps, Scavenger hopped out of the hedge on to the pathway in front of them.

'Sorry to startle you,' he smiled. 'What brings you to man's place?'

Realising this was who had been following them, Fang approached the stranger and told him: 'We're on our way to the Land of Sinna.'

Scavenger laughed a wheezy little laugh that made his shoulders shake, and said: 'You'll be on your way to nowhere if you're not careful. You're in man's place now, you know, and it's full of dangers.'

'We must have taken a wrong turn somewhere,' said Black Tip. 'It's difficult without the brush to guide us.'

'The brush is that way,' said Scavenger, pointing his nose across the river.

Looking up over the water, the others could see that the clouds were now clearing to reveal the running fox in the sky, and they realised that they had been going in the wrong direction. Old Sage Brush and Black Tip were anxious to get back on the right course as soon as possible. Scavenger, however, could see they were in no fit condition to continue, and so he offered to take them to a safe place, a place where, he assured them, neither man nor his fun dogs could touch them, and where they could eat and rest until they were well enough to travel. Then he would guide them back out of his territory. It was an offer they were glad to accept.

Scavenger led them back across some fields to a spot where he judged it safe to await the right time to move. For what seemed a long time, they watched the running fox in the sky play hide and seek behind the clouds. They talked of food, of man and his fun dogs, and of course, about their beloved Beech Paw and the Land of Sinna. Scavenger listened, but the others got the feeling that he wasn't unduly impressed. As far as he was concerned, he had been born and bred in man's place, and there was nowhere like it – certainly not in the country.

At last the distant sound of fun dogs died down, and Scavenger rose to lead them to a safer place. Quickly they ran along the river, past the horses and under a stone bridge, until they came to a series of waterfalls. There they made their way across two wooden beams and out through a narrow gateway in a low stone wall. Now, they found, they really were in man's place. The streets were empty. Yet it was all new to them and very frightening. The smells of man and his machines and his uncollected rubbish were everywhere. They saw a mongrel scraping among a pile of black plastic bags of refuse. Fortunately he was too occupied with his search for food to notice them moving swiftly past the church and through the flashing lights.

Around the corner, Scavenger led them across a road and into the comparative safety of a gently-sloping park. At the foot of this they swam across a wide, fast-flowing river, continued along the bank for some distance, crossed another road, and nipped in through a small iron gate set in a long, high stone wall.

A chill wind was blowing through a row of Austrian pines just inside the wall as Scavenger led them up the hill into a small wood of birch trees whose silvery bark sparkled in the light of the moon. From there he took them across a large flat field dotted with tall white posts, through more woods and finally in between green railings to an area of thick undergrowth.

'Now,' he panted, 'you can rest. No one will trouble you here.'

From the Grand Canal at Inchicore, the foxes had crossed the River Liffey to the Phoenix Park, and were now in the grounds of the President's House, Áras an Uachtaráin.

TWELVE

Creatures Great and Small

A handsome jay flew into a clearing and settled rather jerkily on a stone. For a moment it lifted its crested head and stared at the foxes lying in the undergrowth. With a flash of its bright blue wing feathers, it retreated, perched on an ivy-covered bough for another quick glance at its visitors, and disappeared. In the branches above, two jackdaws sitting side-by-side like love birds, also viewed the unusual sight of so many foxes with considerable interest.

The sun was rising now and its rays were reaching into the undergrowth. Everywhere ivy was sprouting up through the thick carpet of dead leaves, and Vickey could detect the scent of winter flowers on the grassy bank beyond the trees. Beyond that, in fields bounded by white railings, flocks of starlings and wood-pigeons walked hither and thither, busily picking up what food they could for breakfast.

'It's so quiet and peaceful,' said She-la almost absentmindedly.

Scavenger, who over-heard her, laughed.

167

As a hardy little fox who spent most of his time pitting his wits against man and his fun dogs, he found the idea of someone thinking that the city was quiet and peaceful highly amusing.

'Why do you laugh?' asked Vickey. 'Will man hunt us here?'

Scavenger shook his head. 'You're safe here.'

'Aren't there choking hedge-traps?' asked Sinnéad.

'Not here,' said Scavenger.

'What about fun dogs?' asked Fang, rising and coming over to them.

'Very few,' Scavenger told him. 'Man keeps them out.'

He motioned towards the big house with his nose and added: 'I sometimes see two small ones over there, but they just seem to be pets. They never bother me.'

'Are there any shooters?' asked Vickey, mindful of her experience in the meadow back at Beech Paw.

'No, no shooters,' said Scavenger. 'You've nothing to fear in here.'

Old Sage Brush had been lying alongside Black Tip listening to the conversation. 'You haven't said anything about food,' he remarked to Scavenger. 'And what about the strange sounds I can hear on the wind?'

'There's some food all right. Birds, frogs, that sort of thing. But they don't keep any chickens here, or ducks. That's why I have to go out at gloomglow to man's place.'

'I saw no chickens there either,' said Black Tip.

'There are none. But there are plenty of chicken bones and meat if you search around for it and avoid the fun dogs.'

'Where?' asked Hop-along.

'On the streets, in bags, places like that.'

'You mean man's rubbish?' asked Sinnéad. The idea disgusted her.

'Why not?' said Scavenger. 'Man throws away more than he can eat. It's just a matter of picking it up when the fun dogs aren't looking.'

'But how do you survive?' asked Vickey. 'As you said yourself, man's place is full of dangers.'

'It is,' said Scavenger rather cockily, 'but you get used to it, and it's nice to come back here.'

It was a way of life that obviously didn't appeal to the country foxes who liked wide open spaces as far away from man as possible, and fresh food caught in the wild, or when man wasn't looking. Old Sage Brush was still cocking an ear to the wind. 'You haven't told me what those strange noises are. I seem to hear the sounds of birds, or cats, only they're not the sort of sounds I've heard before.'

The others listened intently. The lack of

sight had increased the old fox's hearing immensely, and it was only now as they stopped talking and turned an ear to the wind that they could make them out too – faint noises – but they were there.

'It comes from the Land of the Giant Ginger Cats,' Scavenger told them.

'The what?' asked Skulking Dog, rising to his feet.

'The Land of the Giant Ginger Cats,' Scavenger repeated, and sensing that he might have alarmed them, added: 'Don't worry, they can't harm us.'

'Why not?' asked Fang.

'They're in pens. It's a sort of a farm, but it's not like any you've ever hunted on.'

'Tell us about it,' said Black Tip.

'Well, to start with, the ginger cats are ten feet long.'

The others laughed, and Skulking Dog said: 'I suppose there are giant mice as well?'

'There are,' said Scavenger. 'Bigger than rats. Bigger than fun dogs. Bigger than anything you've ever seen before.'

Thinking of the distorted images he had seen in the aluminium reflectors, Skulking Dog said: 'It must be some sort of trick.'

'It's no trick,' Scavenger assured him. 'They're the same shape and colour as ordinary mice. The only difference is that they're huge and they carry their cubs in a pouch on their bellies.'

170

They all laughed at that, especially the vixens.

'That's a good one,' said Vickey. 'I wish we had a pouch like that.'

'Yes,' said She-la, 'maybe we could take our cubs to safety quicker.'

'But Scavenger,' said Sinnéad seriously, 'there's no such thing.'

'There is,' he asserted, 'and more. There are birds ten feet tall, and horses with humps.' He leaned closer to emphasise what he was saying. 'There are creatures that have necks so long they can eat leaves from the treetops without even stretching ... and there are some with noses so long they can eat off the ground without even bending.'

'What about foxes?' asked Black Tip. 'Are there any giant foxes?'

Scavenger shook his head. 'Foxes aren't allowed there.'

'Why not?' asked Hop-along.

'I don't know. All I know is that foxes aren't allowed there.'

'Where do these giant animals get their food?' asked Fang.

'From man.'

'Oh! I might have known,' said Hop-along. 'That's why there are no foxes.'

'But are you telling us that man feeds these creatures?' asked Black Tip.

'That's right. I've often watched man giving them meat and fish and all sorts of things.'

Old Sage Brush had listened to all this without saying anything. He too was trying to understand what Scavenger was telling them. Unlike the others, however, it wasn't the idea of the giant animals that stuck in his mind.

'What about the birds?' he said. 'I also hear the sounds of birds on the wind – ducks, if I'm not mistaken?

'There are many birds,' Scavenger told him. 'But they're not like the ones you know. They're all shapes and sizes, and some are the colour of the grass, some the colour of the sky. Some are even the colour of the wide eye of gloomglow.'

'The ducks,' repeated Old Sage Brush. 'What about the ducks? Are there many of them?'

'More than you've ever dreamed of. Beyond the wire where the giant animals live, there are lakes, and the water and the islands are full of ducks, and moorhen, and geese, and...' Scavenger paused. 'I just couldn't describe it.'

'Have you ever been in there?' asked Black Tip.

'A few times. But man chased me when I went after the ducks, and put up stronger wire where I got in.'

'Why does man chase us the way he does?' asked She-la. 'Is it just because we kill his chickens and ducks?'

'Well, that's why he chased me from the

lakes,' said Scavenger. 'But there's another reason.'

'What?' asked She-la.

'You wouldn't believe it if I told you. I'll show you before you set off again for the Land of Sinna.'

Leaving She-la, and indeed the others, to think about that, Scavenger returned to the subject of the ducks. He told Old Sage Brush he had prised back a corner of the wire fence not far from a tall beech tree, but had found it too jagged to squeeze in through, and had given up. He had now succeeded in pulling a piece of board from a section of wooden fence on the other side of this strange farm, and was planning to go in that way at the first opportunity.

'If some of us go with you,' said Black Tip, 'we can get enough food for all of us.'

Scavenger shook his head. 'You're in no condition to go.'

'Then, we'll go,' said Sinnéad.

'But you can't,' said Skulking Dog. 'You're in cub.'

'Even so,' Sinnéad replied, 'my cubs are still small within me, and I can hunt as well as any dog fox.'

'And me,' said She-la.

'Maybe you two can, but not me,' said Vickey. 'My cubs are growing heavy.' She turned around and went off into the undergrowth.

Sensing that Vickey had suddenly become uneasy, Black Tip followed her. Old Sage Brush and Skulking Dog had reservations about Sinnéad's suggestion. 'You've just escaped from man,' Skulking Dog reminded her. 'You don't want to risk being caught again.'

'I'll be all right,' Sinnéad assured him. 'You stay here and look after the others.'

Hop-along hobbled over to She-la. He didn't want to risk losing his mate either, and he wasn't happy about the thought of her going out to hunt for him.

'Are you sure there are no shooters in this place you speak of?' Old Sage Brush asked Scavenger.

'None,' replied the little fox.

'At least that's something,' said Fang. 'What's to stop them getting back out?'

'Man has his ways,' said Old Sage Brush. 'No, I don't like it.'

'What don't you like?' asked She-la.

'If man closes the wooden fence, you'll be trapped,' said the old fox. 'Just the way Sinnéad and myself were trapped in the sand-pit.'

'Unless,' said Fang, 'we could do what we do now when we dig an earth – give them another way out.'

This seemed to satisfy Old Sage Brush, and after some consideration, he nodded, saying: 'Okay. Skulking Dog, you can go to the beech tree, and try and enlarge the hole Scavenger has made in the wire fence. Scavenger, you and the vixens can keep yourselves fresh for the raid. If the wire fence doesn't provide a way in, at least it will give you another way out.'

The weather continued to be very changeable. A morning that promised a touch of spring, turned cloudy and by afternoon rain was coming down steadily from a dark grey sky. Behind the green railings, the starlings flocked on to the roof of the big house and the wood-pigeons sheltered in the trees. The finches and the sparrows perched on the lower branches and shuffled miserably, and in the undergrowth below them, the foxes curled up and waited.

Snuggling in beside Black Tip, Vickey now confided in her mate that she was again worried about Old Sage Brush.

'What happens if he can't continue?' asked Vickey. 'If he can't make it back home to Beech Paw? We couldn't go on and leave him. Hop-along's finding the going hard too.'

'Don't worry yourself,' said Black Tip. 'The old fox is tougher than you think. As long as he can move he'll keep going. And Hop-along will be all right. She-la has turned out to be a great strength to him.' While saying this, Black Tip realised that Vickey's concern about the other two also reflected a deeper and more personal concern, so he asked: 'But what about you? Will you be all right?'

Vickey didn't answer right away. Then she said: 'I thought we'd be back in Beech Paw by now. Instead we're here in man's place. Oh, Black Tip, I don't want our cubs to be born here.'

'Neither do I,' Black Tip assured her, 'and don't worry, they won't. We'll leave for Beech Paw tonight.'

Scavenger's original intention was to go after the ducks at gloomglow. But the heavy rain, the failing light, and their increasing hunger changed that. Man, he had noticed, didn't like the rain, and would have gone away leaving the place where the ducks were, deserted. Skulking Dog could now start working at the wire fence as there would be no one around there either. Later, when the giant ginger cats were bellowing for their food, and the keepers were inside getting it ready, they could move in on the ducks with safety.

Old Sage Brush agreed that this was a good plan. With a bit of luck they would have an early supper.

Soon the sounds of hungry animals could be heard clearly. It was nothing new to Scavenger, but the others had never heard anything like it before, and they found it frightening. It took Skulking Dog all the courage he could muster to continue tugging at the wire fence only a few feet from the largest ginger cat he had ever seen. Scavenger hadn't exaggerated one little bit. Up and down its pen the huge animal prowled, great growls coming from deep down its massive throat.

Realising it wouldn't be long now until the animals were fed, Scavenger came along to tell Skulking Dog that the time had come to make their move. Skulking Dog assured him he was making progress, and off the little fox went with the two vixens to the spot where he had made the gap in the wooden fence.

There was no one around, and he quickly hopped through. Not knowing what danger they faced inside, the vixens hopped in too. On the other side of the fence, they followed a path until they came to a high hedge. The hedge consisted of two rows of beech, and they could see that the brown leaves of last year still clinging to it would give them the cover they needed. Following close on Scavenger's heels, they nipped into the hedge and ran along underneath it.

The vixens also found that Scavenger hadn't been exaggerating. There, larger than life, were horses with humps, long-necked creatures eating leaves from the tree-tops, and another with a nose that hung down to the ground. Neither the camels, the giraffes, nor indeed the elephant, spotted the visitors, and so they passed unnoticed up around the back of the elephant house. From there Scavenger led the vixens in a quick dash down towards the lakes, using the cover of any walls or hedges they could find. At one spot the vixens paused, mesmerised by the sight of large blue pheasants in a pen. They had never seen pheasants like them before.

'Hurry,' whispered Scavenger urgently, 'before we're caught.'

Seconds later they were peeping out from behind the home of the grey squirrels. Now they were within sight of the lakes. The squirrels were curled up on a branch, unaware of what was happening. However, someone else was quick to spot the intruders. Below the squirrels, a tiny creature peeped out from under a hollow log. He was a wide-eyed, sharp-eared little mouse who had scraped out two entrances to his home, and had got into the habit of darting from one to the other to see what food visitors had brought and to retrieve an occasional nut when the squirrels weren't looking. It was with great curiosity that he watched the foxes steal away towards the lakes.

Again the vixens found that Scavenger hadn't exaggerated. They came upon the biggest mice they had ever seen with pouches for their young just as he had said, and no sooner had they got over the surprise of that, than they were face to face with the giant ginger cats growling fiercely as they paced to and fro behind a high fence.

Whatever about the wallabies, the lions were more interested in getting food, and scarcely glanced at the foxes as they nipped over into the undergrowth on the side of the lake. There Scavenger paused so that they could take their bearings. Above them they could see the tall beech tree and they wondered how Skulking Dog was getting on. In fact, he was still struggling furiously with the wire fence to make sure they had another escape route, and his activity so close by was making the tiger quite agitated.

Availing of whatever cover he could find, Scavenger led the vixens along the water's edge until they were opposite an island that was covered with trees and thick undergrowth. A quick look around to make sure they hadn't been spotted, and they swam across.

In an oak tree on the far side of the lake, a raccoon which had been watching them out of a corner of his eye, curled up and went back to sleep.

The noise of this strange collection of animals and birds was so loud now the vixens found it very frightening. Scavenger assured them this was just what they wanted. When they pounced on the ducks, no one would notice. He was right. No one did. One alert keeper looked out towards the lake thinking for a moment he saw a sudden movement, but dismissed it as another of the squabbles seagulls were always having as they swooped on pieces of floating food.

As the foxes settled down on the island to a supper of the most exotic duck they had ever tasted, the keepers went about the job of feeding the many animals and birds that couldn't fend for themselves. At long last a contented silence descended on the lake. Animals rested on full stomachs and the only thing that disturbed the peace was the patter of rain on the water.

Because of the rain, the light was fading fast. There was no sign of the keepers, and Scavenger decided the moment had come to strike again. This time, however, he misjudged the situation. Hearing the commotion on the island as ducks and geese and many other lake birds scattered in panic, the keepers realised at once that a fox had got in. It wasn't the first time it had happened, and knowing the damage a fox could do, they stopped what they were at and dashed down to the lake.

Realising his mistake, Scavenger told the vixens to stay where they were. Taking a tight grip on his duck, he swam across to the far shore.

'There he is,' cried a keeper. 'After him.'

This, of course, was what Scavenger wanted. As he ran back up towards the wooden fence where he had got in, She-la and Sinnéad swam the short distance from the other side of the island, and carried their ducks up towards the tall beech tree.

Away on the far side of the zoo, Scavenger slipped back out through the wooden fence before the keepers could catch him, and made a quick dash for the safety of the undergrowth beyond the green railings where Old Sage Brush and the others were waiting.

Meanwhile, She-la and Sinnéad, with Skulking Dog's help had squeezed out through the wire fence. And so their flight from the lake went unnoticed. Unnoticed, that is, by anyone except a raccoon curled up in a ball of fur in an oak tree near the lake, and perhaps, just perhaps, a wide-eyed sharp-eared little mouse looking out from beneath a hollow log in the home of the grey squirrels. Nothing happened in that part of the zoo that they didn't know about.

THIRTEEN

Under the Evergreens

Darkness came and with it the cold. The rain turned to sleet, and the sleet turned to snow. In a dry stone ditch in the grounds of the big house, the foxes curled up in the shelter of the ivy and tangled undergrowth and enjoyed the proceeds of their raid on the zoo.

Later, as the snow clouds cleared, and moonlight sparkled on the whitened fields beyond the trees, Scavenger could see that while the others dozed Vickey was restless, so he went over to her. As he settled down beside her, she thought he really was the skinniest, mangiest little dog fox she had ever seen. Cheeky too, but a likeable rogue.

'We'll be going soon now, Scavenger,' she whispered. 'Why don't you come with us?'

Scavenger licked his lips and shook his head. 'I wouldn't know what to do. I mean, I'd be lost in the country, just the way you're lost here.'

'But surely you can't enjoy living here – in man's place.'

'What makes you say that?'

Vickey shifted uncomfortably. She was afraid she might say something that would hurt his feelings. 'Well, I mean, where will you go after this? You've had good hunting this time, but you can't go back there for a while.'

'True, but there are other places.'

'With big animals?'

'No, no. But there are other wooded places with small birds and frogs and rats, and I know where there's another lake with lots of ducks. I go to a different place each night.'

'But how do you eat the disgusting stuff that man leaves out?'

'I wish there was more of it.'

'You mean you actually like it?'

'Of course I do. You never know what you're going to find. It beats hunting any time.'

'What I can't understand,' said Vickey, 'is how you stand the smell.'

Scavenger gave the funny little wheezy laugh that made his shoulders shake. 'What smell? When I go down into man's place the only thing I can smell is food.'

'Maybe you've been here too long and don't notice it.'

Scavenger smiled. 'Maybe so, but things aren't so bad that I have to leave it to learn the secret of survival.'

Vickey knew she had no answer to that.

'Gloomglow's here,' she observed, changing the subject. 'It's time we were getting on back to Beech Paw. I just hope Old Sage Brush can make it. He's not able for all this travelling you know.'

'You worry too much,' said Scavenger. 'There's plenty of life left in the old dog yet. Let him sleep for a while. Later, when it's safe, I'll take you all back out of man's place and see you safely on your way to Beech Paw. And it might be a good idea if you got some sleep too while you can.'

'Scavenger,' mumbled Vickey before she dozed off.

'What?'

'You promised to tell us why man kills foxes the way he does.'

'And so I will, when the time comes. Now go to sleep.'

The scattering of snow was crisp on the sparse grass as Scavenger led his country cousins back out through the green railings of the big house, across the flat field with the white posts, and into the small wood of birch trees. To their left they could see the silhouette of tall buildings, church spires, and two long chimneys gushing smoke into the night sky. It was still dark, but sounds from man's place indicated a stirring of life, and so they hurried on. However, they didn't leave by the small iron gate. Instead, Scavenger took them away along the high stone wall, and up through the park until they came to a massive double gate at the end of a roadway. Squeezing through, they crossed the road and a few minutes later found themselves at the river. They swam across at a point where the banks were flat and the flow of the water wasn't too strong, and continued on up-river. By now the sounds of man had receded. Nothing disturbed the stillness, except the rushing water and the crackle of the snow on the grass as they trotted along.

Before leaving man's place completely however, Scavenger took them up through the fields to a cluster of houses. 'Now,' he whispered, 'if you want to find out why man kills foxes, stay close and keep quiet.'

Creeping up to a gap in a wall, they peered out across the road. In the lighted window of a shop they could see three women. The women looked back, at them with unseeing eyes and didn't move. Feeling the others freeze, Old Sage Brush asked Black Tip what was wrong.

'Fox furs,' exclaimed Black Tip. 'They're wearing fox furs!'

It was a sight that rooted them to the spot. All they could do was stand and stare, wide-eyed, open-mouthed and unbelieving. The model in the centre was dressed in a coat of fox furs, and around her neck she wore a complete fox skin. The legs hung limply from her shoulders, and a fine head that once had been cunning and free was clasped lifeless across the base of the tail.

Vickey shivered and looked at her own fur. She hadn't noticed before how tatty it had become with the onset of the breeding season. Now as she looked again at the hapless fox in the shop window, she felt uneasy. So did they all, and they thought to themselves that they much preferred to take their chances in the open countryside and leave man's place with all its unpleasant sights and smells to man.

Scavenger led them farther along the river. Then, turning his back to it, he took them across the fields until they came to the canal where he had first met them. This seemed to form the edge of his territory, and in the fields beyond he wished them a safe journey back to the Land of Sinna – and Beech Paw.

'Are you sure you won't change your mind?' asked Black Tip.

'Yes do,' urged Vickey. 'Come with us.'

'If you don't,' said She-la, 'you might end up like that fox we saw around the woman's neck.'

Scavenger laughed his wheezy little laugh until his shoulders shook, and looking down at his own mangy fur, told them: 'Nobody would want this old coat to keep them warm. I can hardly keep warm in it myself.'

Old Sage Brush smiled. 'Scavenger,' he

186

said, 'take care of yourself. That fur of yours may not be worth much to man, but it's worth a lot to us. Don't let them catch you.'

The moon was casting a soft light across the hills and finding a faint reflection in the still waters of the lakes below. From a patch of gorse on the hillside where they lay, Vickey looked up at the stars. The running fox in the sky was almost directly above her head, and had now turned over on its back. It seemed to have stopped running and she knew that it would soon be time they stopped running too.

Not long after leaving man's place, Old Sage Brush had called an unexpected halt, and Black Tip had led them to an earth in a dry bank. Behind the bank a plantation of evergreens stretched back across the hill like a carpet of Christmas trees. The badgers that had dug the earth had chosen well. It gave a good view of the hillside and any danger that came from there, while at the same time providing an escape route up through the trees at the back. The plantation and its undergrowth might also provide food.

Black Tip, his neck still sore from the choking hedge-trap, rolled over on his back so that he could also look up at the running fox in the sky.

'What are you thinking?' Vickey asked him. 'It's lying on its back, just like me.'

'That's what I was thinking,' said Vickey. 'It's stopped running, and soon, so must we.'

Black Tip made no reply. He knew she was right. He also knew something else but couldn't find it in his heart to tell her.

'We never did find the Great White Fox,' Vickey remarked. 'I don't understand it really.'

Black Tip rolled back on his belly and looked at her. 'There's a lot we don't understand,' he told her. 'But we will understand it all in time.' He nudged her affectionately, and added: 'Come on, let's join the others.'

Hearing Black Tip and Vickey talking with Hop-along and She-la, Old Sage Brush came out the back tunnel into the plantation. He paused to stretch the aches of sleep from his body and joined them. Skulking Dog and Sinnéad came up out of the earth a few minutes later, and Fang who had been hunting among the evergreens, arrived shortly afterwards. They lay in a circle around the old fox, waiting to hear what he had to say. A thick layer of last year's needles formed a soft brown carpet and provided them with a rare sense of comfort.

Apart from a wood-pigeon cooing somewhere in the distance, the birds were still silent. Perhaps they were aware of the visitors, or perhaps they preferred other haunts. Whatever the reason, the foxes found the plantation very quiet and peaceful.

As they lay around Old Sage Brush, they listened to the wind and looked up at the tree-tops, tall and slim, swaying gently against the spreading dawn. Then they turned to the old fox expectantly. When he didn't say anything, Sinnéad asked: 'What worries you Sage Brush?'

'There is much to worry all of us,' he replied.

'What?' asked Vickey sitting up with a start. 'We're on our way to Beech Paw. What is there to worry about?'

'The fun dogs,' Old Sage Brush reminded her. 'They still lie between us and Beech Paw.'

'But we can't let them stand in our way,' cried Vickey. 'Not now.'

The old fox sighed. 'Maybe I was wrong to think I could show you the secret of survival. Maybe we shouldn't have left Beech Paw.'

'Of course you weren't wrong,' Black Tip assured him. 'Anyway, we asked you, remember?'

'That's right,' said Fang. 'It was our idea in the first place. And we have learned much.'

The others agreed.

'But have we learned enough to get Vickey back to Beech Paw?' the old fox asked. 'If we press on, we'll have to face the fun dogs, and we can't hope to beat them again. If we stay here, there's a danger we'll get snowed in. Either way, we lose time, and time is something Vickey can't afford.'

'Maybe we should press on,' suggested She-la. 'The fun dogs might not see us.'

'But I've seen *them*,' said Black Tip. 'Or at least their tracks, and sooner or later they'll see ours.'

'What are we to do then?' asked Vickey anxiously.

Old Sage Brush shook his head.

'Let me draw them off,' urged Black Tip.

'And me,' said Skulking Dog.

Old Sage Brush shook his head again. 'Your vixens need you.'

'They don't need me,' said Fang. 'I could go.'

'Fang,' said the old fox, 'you have served me well. You have been my strength when I had none. You have been my courage when I was weak. But I cannot let you go out and draw the fun dogs upon yourself. You'd never out-run them.'

'I could try,' urged Fang. 'I just might make it.'

'No,' said Old Sage Brush firmly. 'I cannot let you risk your life again. We must think of some other way. In the meantime, we must eat.'

The old fox sent Black Tip and Skulking Dog out to hunt, and they hurried off through the evergreens, stopping every now and then to sniff the wind and listen for any sounds that might signal the approach of the fun dogs, or provide a promise of food.

The plantation gave them an entirely different feeling from the one they had in the wide open spaces of the fields. Somehow it gave them a feeling of isolation, and as they looked up at the brightness beyond the swaying tree-tops, a feeling of being surrounded by a bigness they couldn't quite comprehend. It was a strange experience, even for foxes, to watch a stream and not hear it. They came across several such streams, flowing quietly across a bed of needles. There were also dry ditches in the plantation, and from one a large hare sprang out and sped away through the trees. They didn't pursue it. It was going too fast, and anyway, they still hadn't forgotten about Hop-along's encounter with Lepus.

Although generally referred to as pine, the evergreens were in fact spruce, except for those around the edge of the plantation. There, a belt of larch trees shone bare and bright in the wintry sun. The larch looked dead, but it was just that they of all the conifers, shed their foliage in winter, and Black Tip and Skulking Dog could see as they emerged from underneath their graceful branches, that they too were greening now with tiny tufts of neat new needles. It was another reminder that time was running

191

out for Vickey, and they must hurry.

Suddenly they met a stream of young rabbits fleeing from a warren on the grassy bank at the edge of the plantation. The rabbits were terror-stricken and ran right into them. As they plucked two of them from their mad flight, a stoat emerged from the warren. The little hunter stood up on his hind legs, and seeing that the foxes had reaped the benefit of his efforts, bounded forward snarling and squeaking its annoyance. Black Tip and Skulking Dog didn't stop to argue, but streaked off through the trees with their kill.

Having left the rabbits back at the earth for the others, the two resumed their hunting. This time they tried the fields alongside the plantation, but it soon became obvious that the activities of the stoat had driven most other wild life into cover.

Half a dozen magpies swooped on them as they made their way across the fields. They ignored them. The magpies, recognising natural enemies and never lacking courage in the presence of either dog or fox, swooped again. The two foxes continued on their way as if the magpies were no more than midges flitting around their ears. The magpies came in again, closer this time. The foxes turned and sprang at them. Black Tip caught one and the others retreated to the safety of a nearby ash tree. Black Tip smiled, and Skulking Dog guessed what he was thinking. As Old Sage Brush would say, courage was no substitute for cunning. The magpie tasted good – not as good as a chicken or a pheasant, remarked Skulking Dog, but enjoyable nevertheless.

Rising to survey the hillside below them, they could see a farmer glancing at the sky and turning his collar up against the wind. It had been a difficult year for farmers everywhere. Late frosts and continuing snow had brought heavy lambing losses, and they had been slow to sow their wheat. More snow was also the last thing they wanted.

Black Tip turned to go when a movement down at the farmhouse caught his eye. 'Look,' he said, 'it's a fox.'

'But what is it doing there in broad daylight?' wondered Skulking Dog. He thought of the narrow escape he himself had had at the chicken farm shortly after leaving Beech Paw, and added: 'It's asking for trouble.'

Black Tip nodded, and Skulking Dog continued: 'It looks like ... but it couldn't be...'

Black Tip sprang forward, his body trembling. He too had sensed something familiar in the movement of the fox down at the farmhouse. It was Vickey.

FOURTEEN

Alone Against the Wind

A pair of dark brown eyes, sharper even than those of a fox watched Vickey enter the farmyard. They saw her approach the body of a stoat lying on the cement floor of an open barn. Unaware that she was being watched, she sniffed the stoat and turned it over with a nudge of her nose. She didn't see or hear the ghostly white form that swooped on her, until its razor-sharp talons gave her a swift clout on the side of the head. She screamed in a mixture of pain and surprise, and turned her head to see the barn owl come to roost on a rafter.

Unknown to Vickey, she had come upon the object of a bizarre game often played by the owl and two other occupants of this farmyard. The man and woman who lived there had no children, and the light of their lives was a long-haired, black and tan tom-cat and a small brown and white terrier. They lavished on them all the care and attention they would have lavished on children, if they had had any. They fed them choice pieces of meat, and encouraged them to sleep in wicker baskets in the warm kitchen. As a result, the cat had grown to an enormous size and the terrier had become round and fat. Because they got all the food they wanted in the house, they didn't have to hunt, but they did. In fact, hunting was their favourite game. It occupied most of their days, and they had become very good at it. They were renowned in the district for the fact that they could better that fearless little hunter, the stoat, although no one knew how. They also hunted small birds and mice, and whether the hapless victim they brought back to the farmyard was a dead stoat or a half-dead bird, they would spend hours playing with it. It was a game the old hen owl always watched, for when the other two finally tired of it she would swoop on their victim and carry it off. Thus she objected to Vickey's interference, and when she landed on the rafter she screeched a warning to her two friends.

Black Tip and Skulking Dog, who had come as close to the farmyard as they dared, had seen the owl attacking Vickey, but were powerless to do anything. They also saw the great shaggy tom-cat and the terrier dashing out of the house and chasing her. However, it was only a short chase. These two were well aware that a fox could easily out-run them. Moreover, as the owl knew from experience, they still hadn't finished with the stoat, and now that something else had shown an interest in it, they felt like resuming their game.

Relieved that Vickey had got away, Black Tip and Skulking Dog watched the cat and dog returning to the body of the stoat. Round and round it the little terrier hopped, barking loudly as if he expected it to spring at him, until suddenly the cat leapt in and seized it by the throat. A few shakes, and it was the terrier's turn again. All the time, the owl watched and waited. Her turn would come later.

Leaving the stoat hunters to their grisly game, Black Tip and Skulking Dog joined Vickey as she drew abreast of them and took her back to the safety of the earth up in the plantation. None of them rebuked her for what she had done, and she offered no explanation for her strange behaviour. There was no need. They all knew the reason. The cubbing mood was coming upon her, and she was not really to blame. They also realised it was more important than ever now that they should move on to Beech Paw, a point Old Sage Brush was quick to make when Vickey had gone below ground.

'Do you think the stoat hunters will come looking for us?' asked Hop-along.

'They might,' said the old fox. 'Or they might just come across us when they're after stoats. Either way, it's an added danger.'

'We have nothing to fear from a cat,' said Fang.

'But the cat is very big and hunts with a fun dog,' Skulking Dog reminded him. 'They could be a danger to some of us.'

'And the small fun dogs are the worst,' Sinnéad pointed out. 'They can follow us into the earth.'

'Sinnéad's right,' announced Old Sage Brush. 'We can't run the risk of being trapped. We'll have to make a move. But how are we going to get past the fun dogs?'

If the old fox was expecting some of them to come up with the answer, he didn't get it, so he suggested that they apply their minds to it as a matter of urgency, and despatched Fang and Hop-along to get more food. Black Tip could keep an eye on Vickey, and Skulking Dog would give them the extra protection they might now need.

Always conscious of the rather distinctive tracks he left and his inability to run very fast, Hop-along was quick to notice that he and Fang didn't leave any track on the thick carpet of needles that covered the ground beneath the trees. This he found very comforting, and told Fang so. They paused to examine the cones that were scattered everywhere. Fang held one of the longer spruce cones between his front paws and gnawed it with his long teeth, while Hop-along tried to crack one of the smaller larch cones. They were dry and brittle, and both soon came to the conclusion that there was no food in them.

Even though they had gone in the opposite direction from where Black Tip and Skulking Dog had hunted, they found little sign of wild-life in the plantation, so they too decided to extend their search to the open fields. There their efforts were rewarded with the capture of a cock pheasant.

As they trotted back up along the dry bank towards the earth, they came across another badger set. Hop-along was carrying the pheasant, and Fang decided to see if the set had been abandoned by badgers and perhaps occupied by rabbits. Hop-along dropped the pheasant and waited. Suddenly there were grunts and squeals from somewhere in the set, and a few moments later he was startled to see Fang sailing through the air and landing at his feet. The set was occupied all right, but by badgers which neither liked the smell nor the living habits of foxes. They weren't going to share their home with any fox, be it Fang or anyone else.

With only his pride injured, Fang gathered himself up and departed from the scene as quickly as possible. Realising what had happened, Hop-along picked up the pheasant and followed him.

When they arrived back at the earth, they

were concerned to hear that Vickey had somehow managed to slip away again. This time she appeared to have gone in the direction of Beech Paw, and Black Tip had gone after her. Knowing the great danger both of them faced, Old Sage Brush sent Fang to help them.

The urge to get home to Beech Paw for her cubbing time had driven Vickey to the point of desperation. Throwing caution to the wind, she had followed her instinct blindly. It is doubtful if she even considered that she or her unborn cubs might be in danger. All she knew was that she must get back, and somehow nothing else seemed to matter.

Foxes give off a much stronger scent as they approach cubbing time, and Black Tip had no difficulty following her. It was obvious where she was heading, and why. Normally, he knew, she would be preparing a nursery for her cubs at this time, and as he raced through the trees after her, he now realised that they had let her down by not getting her back to Beech Paw as promised. He just hoped he would find her before the fun dogs.

Coming to the edge of the evergreens, Black Tip heard a great commotion, and fearing he was too late, cautiously approached the place where the noise was coming from. It was a curious mixture of sound that puzzled him, He recognised the barking of a fox and a small dog, and thought of the ones that ran with the alsatian. But there were other noises which he didn't recognise, and which didn't fit his fears.

Creeping towards a clearing in the trees, it all soon became clear to him. There, on a humpy piece of ground that was riddled with rabbit holes, were the stoat hunters. The great shaggy tom-cat was hissing and pawing savagely at one particular hole, and the terrier was running around, sticking his head down other holes and scratching and barking madly. It soon became apparent to Black Tip that this time their quarry wasn't a stoat. Now and then, he could see the face of a fox, soiled and bloody, eyes wide and terrified, snapping at its tormentors, while in the trees above, the barn owl shuffled and screamed as she watched another game.

Somehow, Black Tip knew, they had cornered Vickey. She had taken refuge in the largest burrow, and he wondered why they didn't go into some of the smaller burrows and flush her out. Either they were too fat, he thought, or they just wanted to tease and torment her. In any event, they had her cornered, and he wondered how he could get her out. Perhaps if he ran close by they would follow him. He found himself doing so even as he was thinking about it, but it was no use. The dog and cat hesitated barely a moment to look at him before continuing with their deadly game of cat and mouse with Vickey.

So worried was Black Tip with Vickey's plight, he could hardly think. He knew from what he had seen down in the farmyard, that the cat and the little fun dog were experts at this game. Few animals could catch a stoat and most preferred not to risk an encounter with one if it could be avoided. These two, however, seemed to enjoy it, and now they had cornered the fox who had dared deprive them of their fun. The fox would do until another stoat came along, and Black Tip knew there was no chance of that, unless... He thought of the little stoat he had seen farther down the plantation while out hunting with Skulking Dog, and wondered if he might somehow be able to use it.

Not quite knowing what he was going to do, Black Tip turned and ran as fast as he could back into the evergreens. A jumble of thoughts flashed through his mind as he streaked through the trees. Where would he find the stoat? And what could he do with it if he did find it? Could he kill it and take it back to the cat and the dog? He had never killed a stoat before, although he had heard of some foxes that could do it. He had always been told they were ferocious fighters for all their size and were not to be tangled with. But what else could he do? He pressed on.

The bank where the stoat had been hunting for rabbits was now deserted. Quickly Black Tip searched the field on the other side of it. No sign of it there either. He scouted around under the trees, and near a pile of logs discovered the stoat face to face with a rat. There was a blur of sinuous bodies, and the rat lay dead, bitten in the back of the neck. Sensing it was being watched, the stoat stood up on his hind legs and looked around, only to duck from the ghostly white shape of the barn owl that had followed Black Tip and silently swooped down over a familiar enemy.

The stoat was annoyed. It didn't like being watched, and it knew the owl would seize the rat if she could. The owl had now perched on a nearby branch, and the stoat made as if to pursue her, but quickly returned to the rat and placed its forepaws on it. The owl screeched and swooped again. The stoat leaped towards her, but missed and received a sharp clout on its head for its trouble. Now it really was angry, and as the owl landed on the branch of another tree, it streaked up the trunk with the speed of a squirrel, determined to get her.

Black Tip knew that the stoat still hadn't seen him, and in that instant he saw his chance. He raced forward, picked up the rat, and made off as fast as he could go. Glancing back, he could see the stoat bounding after him in hot pursuit. It wasn't going to let him get away with it this time.

Approaching the rabbit warren, Black Tip could tell by the barking and hissing that Vickey was still trapped. He saw the owl gliding ahead of him and perching on a branch at the edge of the plantation. The stoat, he knew, wasn't far behind. He paused. He didn't want the owl to get to the rat first. At the last moment, he dropped it and ran. The stoat was on it in an instant. The owl uttered a harsh scream, and the cat and the terrier stopped what they were doing and looked over. Seeing the stoat, they immediately raced towards it.

It was at that moment that Black Tip found Fang beside him, and together they rushed in to get Vickey out. Smeared with blood and stricken with terror, she was a pitiful sight, but the instinct of survival gave her the strength to run. Black Tip and Fang took off after her, and as Black Tip looked back, he could see the cat and the terrier engaging in their favourite game. The terrier was hopping around the stoat like a mongoose around a snake, barking and snapping, while the tom-cat crouched, ready to spring, and the owl watched and waited.

Even in her terror, Vickey had run away from the evergreens in the general direction of Beech Paw, and the two dog foxes knew better than to try and reason with her. At least, they thought, they might be able to keep her out of trouble and help her find a safe place to rest. Suddenly, however, they found themselves being mobbed by a number of rooks. They were trotting along under a row of beech trees that had once sheltered the lonely homestead of a sheep farmer. Perhaps the rooks had memories of foxes or stoats preying on young squabs that fell from their nests. Or perhaps they knew something was wrong. Creatures of the wild are quick to sense when other creatures are in trouble.

Whatever the reason, the rooks continued to mob them until they were well away from the trees. Black Tip thought of how he and Skulking Dog had caught one of the magpies when they were out hunting, and wondered if he might do the same now. The rooks, however, wheeled well out of range.

In a rocky depression some distance away, other eyes looked up at the rooks and wondered what they had found so interesting. The fun dogs had been resting after a sheep-hunting escapade, and sensing from the action of the crows that a stranger had strayed into their territory, they rose to investigate.

The first the foxes knew the fun dogs were searching for them, was when a snipe rose with a shriek from a marshy patch of hillside and spiralled into the sky. Looking back they immediately recognised their old enemies, the alsatian and the three smaller dogs. They were fairly close, and whatever about Black Tip and Fang, it was obvious there was no way Vicky could outrun them.

'There's only one thing for it,' Black Tip told Fang. 'I'll draw them off. You look after Vickey.'

Fang shook his head. 'Your place is with Vickey. I'll go.'

'But your leg,' Black Tip protested.

'It's as good as new,' Fang assured him.

The two dog foxes looked at each other. They had become very firm friends since that day they had fought for the favours of Vickey back at Beech Paw. It was strange how jealousy had turned to resentment, resentment to admiration, and admiration to friendship.

'There's no other way,' added Fang.

Black Tip nodded. 'I wish I could go with you.'

'So do I, but Vickey needs you.'

'You must take great care,' warned Black Tip. 'You'll be up against greater odds than you've ever faced before.'

Fang laughed. 'They'll have to have their wits about them if they want to catch me.'

Black Tip knew Fang was trying to make light of the danger. Then a familiar bark of excitement told them the fun dogs had picked up their scent.

'I'll be off then,' said Fang.

'Take care,' cautioned Black Tip. 'And don't forget, run with the wind.'

A short distance away, Fang stopped and looked back. He saw Black Tip leading Vickey to the shelter of some rocks. The fun dogs hadn't seen them, but their barking was getting louder now. Fang knew he must show himself, otherwise the scent would lead them to Black Tip and Vickey. He made his way across a stony slope. Small stones began to roll down the hill, taking others with them in a noisy stream of rubble. The fun dogs looked up. They saw him. They squealed with excitement and bounded after him. Pausing only long enough to make sure they didn't abandon him and return to the stronger scent of Black Tip and Vickey he turned and sped in the general direction of Beech Paw.

Man wasn't to be seen much in this hill country, and Fang was glad. It was bleak and sparse, but it enabled him to move fast. It was so long since he had been on his own, he was reminded of the days before Beech Paw when he had hunted by himself. Those were good days, he thought, but so were the days with Old Sage Brush and the others. He had enjoyed those too. The adventures had been good, and he had learned a lot. Now they were depending on him. He must not let them down.

The fun dogs were barking loudly as they

launched themselves into the chase. How, Fang wondered, was he going to out-run them? What if the old fox was right and he couldn't? If they killed him, they would surely get the others. Yet he did have the advantage of being on his own. On the way from Beech Paw, they had been delayed by Old Sage Brush and Hop-along, and there was no way they could have out-run the fun dogs. Black Tip's unfortunate tussle with the choking hedge-trap hadn't helped either. Dogs with a taste for blood could read the signs of a tussle like that. It was just as well they hadn't seen Vickey. They'd have sensed she was in trouble, and that would have been the end for her. He had never said it to Black Tip but he still had a great liking for her, and still wished he could have had her for his mate.

The barking of the fun dogs brought him back to reality with a jolt. They were gaining on him. Black Tip's parting words ran through his mind. 'Take care,' Black Tip had said, 'and run with the wind.' It was the same advice Old Sage Brush had given them when they had set out from Beech Paw. The problem was that unless the wind changed direction, he must run into it to make sure the fun dogs followed him. On the other hand, he couldn't risk letting them get too close to him, so he circled with the wind to slow them down and give himself time to think.

He wished Black Tip was with him. What would he do if he was in this situation? He'd do what Old Sage Brush had taught him to do – use his cunning where courage wasn't enough.

Thinking of Black Tip made Fang wonder if the choking hedge-trap had been re-set. Surely it would, since it would have been obvious that a fox had been caught in it. This gave him an idea. He would now use the wind to even greater advantage.

Turning into the wind again. He headed for the area where Black Tip had been caught in the choking hedge-trap. He could hear from the barking that the fun dogs had picked up his scent again and were gaining on him. That was what he wanted. A short time later he found the field and then the hedge where he had struggled to free Black Tip. Just as he had anticipated, the choking hedge-trap was back in position. He paused and looked behind him. He could hear the fun dogs crashing through the gorse at the top of the field. Then they burst out into the open, and on seeing him began barking with greater excitement than ever. Quickly he hopped over the hedge-trap and disappeared from their view.

Unaware that they were running into a trap, the dogs careered down the field and into the gap in the hedge. A loud yelping told Fang his plan had worked. Looking back, he saw the alsatian struggling to free itself. However, he could also see that because of the dog's height, it wasn't its head but its forelegs that had been caught. This meant it would soon free itself and come after him again, but at least he had earned himself a breathing space. He chuckled. Old Sage Brush would have liked that one.

Back at the hedge the alsatian was still struggling on its hind legs to try and free itself from the snare. The smaller dogs were running around, barking, but not knowing what to do.

The snare had tightened at the alsatian's knees. It wrenched its forelegs again. The snare slipped over its knees and down to its paws. Dancing back on its hind legs, it gave a final wrench and was free. Immediately it turned and sped away in pursuit of the fox, followed by its three smaller companions.

Fang knew that the fun dogs wouldn't give up so easily. It wasn't long before he heard them on his trail again, and he was glad. The last thing he wanted was them to give up and turn back. At the same time he realised that he would have to use every trick he had ever learned if he was to stay ahead of them. He circled, doubled back, laid false trails, used streams, everything in fact he could think of. However, as the day wore on, the dogs grew closer. He was wondering what he was going to do, when he came across a badger set. If there were badgers in the area, perhaps there were foxes too. If not, maybe an empty earth where he could take refuge. Desperately he scouted the fields, but search as he would he could find no trace of either fox or earth. Then it occurred to him that the badger set might be empty and he could take refuge there. Again his luck was out. The set was occupied.

Fang was turning to go when he remembered how he had gone into the set back at the evergreens and to his embarrassment and Hop-along's amusement had been booted out by an angry boar. He wondered. The fun dogs were closing in on him. Now they had spotted him. Well, he thought, here goes. Plunging into the set, he whizzed past a badger who had been awakened by the barking of the dogs. The boar was so surprised that Fang was past him before he realised what was happening. Turning around to give chase, the boar found three small dogs piling up at his hind feet. Furious at this invasion of his home, he did what the other badger had done to Fang. He pulled in his back feet and unleashed them with all the power he could muster, catapulting the small dogs clear out of the set to land yelping at the feet of the alsatian.

Fang, meanwhile, had skidded past the boar's mate and her cubs and had gone out a back way with the speed of a scalded cat.

By the time the dogs discovered they had been tricked again, he had gained another head start. He was, however, far from happy. They had come close – too close. He might not be so lucky next time. And he still hadn't succeeded in drawing them away from the path to Beech Paw.

Pausing briefly to take his bearings, Fang could see he was now on the land of the farmer who had fired at Skulking Dog and himself the day they had stopped to feed on the sheep that had been killed by the fun dogs. He hadn't realised he had circled back so far in his efforts to keep ahead of them, and he knew he would have to be very careful. They were familiar with this territory, probably more familiar with it than he was. He'd also have to keep an eye out for the farmer's dogs and a very hostile farmer.

Thinking of these things, it now occurred to Fang that if he was on dangerous ground, so also were the fun dogs, and he wondered if, perhaps, he could turn that to his advantage and get rid of them once and for all. He looked back. They were closing in on him again. It would be dangerous, he thought, but what had he to lose? It was worth a try.

In a field not far from the farm buildings, he could see a flock of sheep, and he streaked towards them. In a moment he was in among them, sending them running, bleating, first as a flock, then in all directions. A few

211

seconds later the fun dogs were in there too. Now they could see him, now they couldn't as he ran hither and thither among the sheep. Not surprisingly, the sheep panicked, and the more they did so, the more excited the dogs became. In their excitement, they soon forgot all about Fang, and their lust for chasing and killing sheep, their pastime for so long, took over. Throwing all caution to the wind, they proceeded to indulge themselves in an orgy of destruction.

Having lured them into the field, Fang now slipped away from it, and when next he stopped it was to listen to the sound of shots from the direction of the farm. He waited to see if the fun dogs would reappear. There was no sign of them, and he turned to go back for Black Tip and Vickey and the others. The way to Beech Paw, he knew, was now clear.

FIFTEEN

When the Hogweed Blooms Again

A late snowstorm was swirling around Glen-sinna, turning the meadows an unseasonal white and giving an edge to the wind that ruffled the rooks in the beech trees. However, the foxes that made their way doggedly along the dry ditch beneath the long row of beeches scarcely noticed it. They were back in their beloved Land of Sinna, and they knew a disused quarry where the snow wouldn't reach and the wind wouldn't worry them.

It seemed a long time since they had left Beech Paw. But the quarry was still unoccupied, the den dry and undisturbed. There they would rest a while before going their separate ways.

As they snuggled close together for warmth, they thought of all they had seen and done. They were tired, and because of their tiredness they wondered among themselves if it had been worthwhile.

Old Sage Brush sighed. 'Why do you have so little faith?' he asked.

They lowered their heads, not knowing

what to reply, and the old fox went on: 'Where is the determination that defeated all who opposed us? Where is the courage that drove back the fun dogs, and where is the cunning that destroyed them? Have you learned so little that you falter now?'

'But have we learned enough to survive the attacks of *man?*' asked Vickey.

Knowing this was what they were all wondering, Old Sage Brush answered with one of those wise sayings that had so often given them courage before.

'Tell me this,' he said. 'If the lowly beetle can overcome the mighty elm, however tall, cannot the cunning of Vulpes overcome the work of man, however great?'

'There are many beetles,' remarked Black Tip, 'and there are only a few of us.'

'True,' replied Old Sage Brush. 'There are few of us, but we are wiser now, and very soon we will be few of many.'

The others were silent, and as always, sorry that they had once again doubted the old fox. They knew this was his way of reminding them that cubbing time was almost upon them, and that the lessons they had learned would help not only themselves, but their cubs, to survive.

Soon they drifted off to sleep, and for the first time in a long while, it was a peaceful sleep. Some of them dreamt of hunting in the fields around Beech Paw again, and some of them dreamt of the cubs they would soon have and how they would teach them to hunt.

As for Old Sage Brush who was dozing beside Vickey and Black Tip, he dreamt they were on their travels from Beech Paw again, and when he awoke he began to think about them. The little brown hen, he recalled. That was their first adventure. He chuckled now as he thought about it. It had worked well, hadn't it? Then he found himself thinking about Lepus, the leader of the hares, and how Hop-along had fooled him. He smiled. That was a good one. So was the way the horses and the howling dogs had been thrown into confusion at the hunt. That was when Skulking Dog and Running Fox had brought his daughter Sinnéad back into his life. Sinnéad and She-la would be telling their cubs about the great raid they had made into the Land of the Giant Ginger Cats with Scavenger. Ah, Scavenger, thought Old Sage Brush. He was a great little fox. In a way he reminded him of Whiskers, the otter. It was good that they had been able to help Whiskers put a stop to the greedy mink. Then the fun dogs had almost put a stop to them. That was a great fight. It was Fang who had finally put a stop to the fun dogs. Faithful Fang. He would be heading off now, but the young foxes would hear all about him. They'd also hear how Black Tip had saved Vickey from the stoat hunters.

Vickey, content now to be back in Beech Paw, would be turning her den into a nursery, and the other vixens would be looking around for dens of their own. It was time.

In a snow-white dawn, Black Tip and Vickey stood with Old Sage Brush on the rim of the quarry. The others had gone their separate ways, and the old fox, back again on familiar ground, was going his. Silently they touched noses, and then he was away.

As they watched him go, Vickey said: 'Do you really think we found the secret of survival?'

'I think so,' said Black Tip. 'Don't you?'

Vickey smiled and nodded.

'But we never did find the Great White Fox,' said Black Tip.

'Maybe not,' Vickey replied. 'Then again, maybe we didn't look hard enough...'

Snowflakes were swirling across the fields, and as they watched Old Sage Brush make his way along the hedgerows, his coat soon became white and he disappeared into the snow-clad countryside.

A gentle breeze, softened by the late onset of spring, ruffled the sparse hair on Vickey's underside as it rose and fell with the breath of contentment. Her two suckling cubs were at one with the world, and so was she. One cub had died within her during the fight with the fun dogs, but the other two more than made up for it. From where she lay she could see that spring had brought forth from the moss, the first fragile shoots of wood-sorrel. Three heart–shaped leaves on a slender pink stem; larger than a shamrock, yet light green and delicate. By the time their small white flowers appeared, she knew her cubs would have opened their eyes. Shifting her gaze to the top of the bank immediately opposite, she could see that while she had been having her cubs, young ferns had been pushing their way up into the world, and now stood with heads curled, like notes of music. Overhead in the brambles, small birds were singing. Nature had written her own symphony to the new life that was springing up all around.

Vickey was contemplating these things when Black Tip arrived. He had caught her some food in the meadows, and as usual she would bury it in a hiding place nearby and eat it later when she was hungry and the cubs were full.

They were both amused by the little dog's black tip.

'No need to ask you what you're going to call him,' smiled Black Tip. 'And what about the vixen? What's her name going to be?'

Vickey caressed the little she-cub. 'Running Fox,' she announced. 'We'll call her Running Fox.'

'Why Running Fox?' asked Black Tip.

'Because we've stopped running, that's why.'

Black Tip was perplexed. 'Why then call her Running Fox?'

'What else?' smiled Vickey. 'It was the great running fox in the sky that guided us in our search for the secret of survival. And I'll never forget little Running Fox in the Land of the Howling Dogs. That was his home and he wouldn't run away from it. And now that we've returned to Beech Paw, we've stopped running, haven't we?'

'We have,' said Black Tip. 'Now, take good care of little Black Tip and Running Fox. I'll see you later.'

From the rim of the quarry, Black Tip surveyed the valley. It was quiet and peaceful. Soon white blooms of cow parsley would spread along the hedgerows like spiders' webs, but not for long. In no time at all they'd give way to the flowering hogweed. And then what? Black Tip smiled wryly to himself. He knew only too well that when the hogweed blooms had come and gone, man would hunt the fox again.

Author's Note

If all the foxes named in this book – Vickey, Black Tip, Fang, Old Sage Brush, Hopalong, She-la, Skulking Dog, Sinnéad, Running Fox and Scavenger – had succumbed to the snare and the gun, they would have provided one person with a fur coat and possibly a hat. But it would not have been a full-length coat, as that requires about fourteen pelts. Fortunately, Vickey and her friends remain free, and in spite of everything the red fox as a species continues to survive.

The threat to it arose in the mid 1970s. Rabies was spreading westward across Europe, and in many areas the fox was falling victim of attempts to bring the disease under control, as it was known to be a carrier. Then in 1977 France increased bounties on foxes as part of an all-out drive to prevent the spread of rabies there. At the same time, long-haired furs had come back into fashion, so the fox was also being hunted intensively for its pelt. In North America, 388,000 red foxes were 'harvested' in 1977–78, while in West Germany the number caught or shot rose from 186,000 to 194,000.

It was about this time that the fur companies also sought supplies from Ireland and Britain which, unlike their European neighbours, were free of rabies. Being a relatively small country, the impact was particularly noticeable in Ireland. Prices quickly rose from the traditional £1 bounty to almost £20 for a pelt. Fox trapping became a lucrative business for many people, and as the trapping continued unabated, fears were expressed for the fox's survival.

Not everyone, of course, agreed that the fox was in danger of being wiped out. Nevertheless, it is known that in 1979–80, the first season in which export licences were required in the Republic of Ireland, 36,500 fox pelts were exported. Another 36,400 were shipped out the following season, and by 1981–82, the number had risen to 40,700. In addition, an estimated 10,000 were being exported annually from Northern Ireland. Ireland, therefore, was in the unusual position of exporting over 50,000 fox pelts in one year. Less than 10,000 of these were farmed. 40,000 were caught in the wild – almost half the number of red foxes trapped in Canada.

Fears were also expressed for the future of the fox in Britain, where it was estimated that Britain and Ireland between them supplied over 100,000 pelts in 1979. In 1982, however, prices began to fall and the trappers became less active. In Ireland, hunts say they noticed an increase in the number of foxes in the 1982–83 season, and that generally there has been a steady improvement.

In spite of the measures taken to control rabies, the French and German authorities noted that the number of foxes in infected areas was growing again.

In Canada, where the trapping of red foxes is controlled in most provinces and territories, the experts say that long-term statistics do not indicate any reduction in numbers, and that nowhere in Canada is the red fox considered threatened.

In the United States concern for maintaining adequate numbers of the red fox during the years of high prices prompted most States in the Midwest – where the majority of those 'harvested' are caught – to impose controls on hunting.

In general, therefore, despite all the odds, the red fox continues to 'run with the wind'. However, I hope it continues to do so, as fur seems to be coming into fashion again.

TOM MCCAUGHREN
2005